ON THE HOLLOWAY ROAD

Unmotivated and dormant, Jack is drawn into the rampant whirlwind of Neil Blake, who he meets one windy night on the Holloway Road. Inspired by Jack Kerouac's famous road novel, the two young men jump into Jack's Figaro and embark on a similar search for freedom and meaning in modern-day Britain. Pulled along in Neil's careering path, taking them from the pubs of London's Holloway Road to the fringes of the Outer Hebrides, Jack begins to ask questions of himself, his friend and what there is in life to grasp. Taking on speed cameras and CCTV, motorway riots and island detours, will their path lead to new meaning or ultimate destruction?

ANDREW BLACKMAN

ON THE HOLLOWAY ROAD

Complete and Unabridged

ULVERSCROFT
Leicester

First published in Great Britain in 2009 by
Legend Press Ltd.
London

First Large Print Edition
published 2010
by arrangement with
Legend Press Ltd.
London

British Library CIP Data

Blackman, Andrew.
   On the Holloway Road.
   1. Male friendship- -Fiction. 2. Automobile travel- -
   Great Britain- -Fiction. 3. Great Britain- -social life
   and customs- -Fiction. 4. Large type books.
   I. Title
   823.9′2–dc22

   ISBN 978–1–44480–018–0

Published by
F. A. Thorpe (Publishing)
Anstey, Leicestershire
Set by Words & Graphics Ltd.
Anstey, Leicestershire
Printed and bound in Great Britain by
T. J. International Ltd., Padstow, Cornwall

This book is printed on acid-free paper

To Genie, with love.

Acknowledgements

My heartfelt thanks to the family of Luke Bitmead, particularly Elaine Hanson and Tiffany Orton for their kindness and generosity.

1

I first met Neil not long after my father died. I was living in a big old red-brick Victorian semi in north London with my mother and her vicious cat Sparky, trying and failing to finish a long, learned novel packed tight with the obscure literary allusions and authentic multicultural credentials that the publishers loved in those days. Then out of nowhere Neil rode into town, all bravado and muscles, shaved head and mad, staring eyes. He was still just a boy, really, but a boy with an ASBO at fourteen, a caution at fifteen, a spell in junior detention at sixteen and with a boy of his own by seventeen. He was a boy who was wild, dangerous and soft-hearted, a boy who read Nietzsche one minute and manga the next, a boy who wanted to learn everything, see everything, do everything, a boy who wanted to live more badly than anyone else I knew.

Compared to my own sad, shambling existence in the shadows of life, his was a kaleidoscope. I peeped from behind my mother's curtains at the world outside and wrote about people like Neil. I never believed that he really existed until I met him.

Here's how it happened. It was one of those long, cold winter evenings in London, when the streets are slick with a rain you don't recall having fallen and the lights are an orange ball above you in the damp, black chill, fighting feebly against the night. Water hangs in the air with nowhere to go and as you brush against these tiny cold needles they stab your face, making you draw your hood closer about you. Long, dark alleyways harbour thieves and villains, furtive drug-dealers, nervous knife-wielders and young drunk couples rutting. Through it all runs the Holloway Road, a long straight road with dismal shuttered shops on either side, the gloom punctuated at infrequent intervals by the bright lights of a pub, kebab shop, curry house, burger joint. One or two of the old fish and chip shops remain, but they are relics of a time fast being forgotten.

A younger crowd roams the streets on these nights, ravenous for real red meat, big slabs of it slathered in ketchup and hot chilli sauce. Fish seems strangely genteel for such a crowd. Even an inch of grease and a side order of thick, stodgy chips cannot hide the slight effeminacy of the tender white fish that melts away at the first bite. The crowd on the Holloway Road these days wants meat that you can bite into, gristle that you can chew on, blood that you can wipe off your lower lip. It wants its beer cold, its curry hot, its lights bright and its music loud. Nothing luke-warm, nothing ambiguous for this crowd.

If you follow the long, straight Holloway Road far beyond the neon horizon, you'll end up in Scotland. It's hard to believe, but this drab parade of tawdriness is the Great North Road by another name. Before too long, the Holloway Road becomes Archway Road, then Aylmer Road, Lyttelton Road, Falloden Way, then the Barnet Bypass and then you're out of the suburbs and into open countryside. Green fields and hedgerows flash past as you tick off the towns — Stevenage, Letchworth, Peterborough, Newark, Doncaster, Pontefract, Darlington, Durham.

Fight your way through the huge smoky grey sprawl of Newcastle and you then find yourself speeding along quiet open roads, close enough to the sea to smell the salt in the air and hear the seagulls cawing but never quite close enough to see that big grey frigid North Sea until suddenly you're past Berwick-upon-Tweed and hopping over the border into Scotland almost without realising it. And there is the sea in front of you — white-topped waves, freezing and forbidding, bordered by craggy crumbling cliffs.

After only a few minutes the road turns away in disappointment and heads inland, cutting across open countryside to grand, regal old Edinburgh, with its magical castle suspended in the clouds above the city.

You skirt over the top of ancient Holyrood Park and, for the last few hundred yards of its existence, the A1 takes on the name of Waterloo Place, as if trying to reassert its Englishness one last time, reminding the burghers of this proud town that the A1 begins on Newgate Street in London, where Rob Roy himself was held in chains.

I was dreaming all these unconnected vague drunken dreams as I sat in a plastic box of light, sound and blood. Donna's Kebabs I think it was called and I was taking refuge from the oppressive damp mist outside which had, after I'd spent some time walking up and down the Holloway Road, pierced the protective film of alcohol and got to my joints, making my elbows and knees ache arthritically. I sat huddled over a white foam box filled with grey-brown, glistening slices of meat, encased in pitta bread and doused in hot sauce, ketchup, mayonnaise, lettuce, tomato, red onion, white onion, cucumber, gherkins and olives. By the time Neil walked in I had left magical castles and folk heroes far behind and was pondering on the olives, a nice touch but not right. I admired the originality, but originality is not what you expect from a kebab house at midnight on the Holloway Road in the middle of November. You want something to fill your stomach with the expected greasy-sweet flavours. The sourness of the olives was a surprise and left me feeling somewhat dissatisfied.

Donna did not have any other customers that night — perhaps others felt the same about olives in a kebab — so I was surprised when this big, shaven-headed hulk of a man ignored all the empty tables and eased himself creaking into the little red plastic chair opposite me. His gruff 'Dja mind?' was uttered far too late to admit any response but an impotent shrug.

For long minutes he said nothing, just attacked his extra large kebab as if he hadn't eaten for a month. I sat saying nothing, eating nothing. I couldn't. I got a sensation that was strange to me at the time but would soon become familiar: that Neil was doing enough living for the two of us, and there was nothing left for me to do but watch. Soon he had ketchup and chilli sauce all over his stubbly chin, and bits of lettuce had flown all over the table, the floor, his jeans, his t-shirt. Whereas I had been eating my kebab using a small folded piece of pitta bread as an ersatz fork,

Neil just shoved the whole bundle of meat, salad and sauce into his face and began chomping with his huge strong jaws. Slashing the food to pieces and somehow ending up with most of it in his mouth, he chewed only perfunctorily before gulping it loudly down and setting those chomping blades immediately to work again.

The noise was astonishing. The dull beat of the radio, the squealing roar of the traffic on Holloway Road, and the underlying buzz of the slowly rotating lump of grizzly meat in the window were all drowned out by the sound of Neil's bones crashing against each other, his saliva washing around among the sauce, ketchup and meat, his muscles working so hard that his temples pulsed furiously with each pincer-like motion of those powerful jaws. His face, already blood-red, became redder with each mouthful and, just as I was beginning to fear that he would choke, he put the remains of the kebab down, took a big slurp of Coke and belched softly.

'So whatcha doing tonight?' he asked. He looked like a child suddenly, all eager energy and bright eyes, waiting for the next amazing thing to come his way.

'I was looking for my friends,' I replied. 'I lost them somewhere back there.' I gestured vaguely over my shoulder into the misty wet darkness, and Neil's eyes followed my arm faithfully, searching the night for people he'd never seen before.

'Can't you call them?' he asked. 'Text them? Page them? Email them? IM them? Photograph yourself holding up a sign saying 'Where the fuck are you?' and send it to them? I mean, who loses people these days?'

I looked down at my kebab and picked up a small mouthful with my piece of pitta bread. 'I don't have a mobile,' I said awkwardly. Usually it was a sentence I pronounced with pride, as it portrayed one of my few truly distinguishing features. People would draw in their breath and regard me with awe, as one who had asserted his individuality and resisted the siren call of technology. But suddenly, that night, my lack of a mobile phone felt like what it really was, an affectation. To my relief and astonishment, Neil did not pass judgement one way or the other, just accepting it baldly as one more simple fact to add to his growing store of knowledge about the world around him.

'Well, if you can't find them, they've either gone home or gone to a club in the centre. Or they just don't want to be found,' he said after a moment of intense concentration. 'So here is what I propose. We'll finish our food here, and then go around the corner to the

Dog's Head and talk to as many people as we can, until we find someone who's going to a party afterwards. Then we tag along and have the time of our lives. How's that sound? By the way, I'm Neil Blake.'

'Jack Maertens,' I replied, and Neil took that for assent to his plan of action, for he began attacking the rest of his kebab and motioned for me to do the same. I did, feeling a little sick a few minutes later as I lurched back out into the dark wet Holloway night and followed Neil to the Dog's Head. It was a dive of the worst kind, so bad that I didn't want to go in until he told me patiently and seriously, as if talking to a slow child, that he had chosen it precisely for the reason of its awfulness, which would make anyone in it naturally keen to get out and on to somewhere better. He was soon proved right, too, as after only a half-hour or so of working that tight-packed smelly young crowd, he hit upon a group of students who were heading to a party up in Highgate. All he had to do was tell them a few jokes and buy a couple of rounds of drinks, which he left me to pay for, and suddenly we were on the night bus chugging up Highgate Hill, where a few hundred years ago Dick Whittington had heard the Bow Bells calling him back to fame and fortune in London, and where today middle-class families drive their huge snorting Landrovers up to huddle together in expensive refuge from the pulsating violent ugliness below.

For Neil and me that night, Highgate Hill was a place of cheap wine in plastic cups, vodka jelly, cheap cigarettes, expensive hashish from a reputable dealer on the Edgware Road, tequila slammers, half-grabbed kisses with a girl on a sofa, loud music, shouting and some attempts to dance.

By the time we left it was already morning and people in suits and raincoats were climbing sourly onto buses. The sun was still not up, though, and neither was my mother when I sneaked in and crept quietly to my room. What had happened to Neil I didn't know, but he must have followed me home because the next day, although I hadn't given him my address or phone number, and was caught between relief and regret over it, I went downstairs and found him there — sitting in my mother's living room sipping a cup of tea, and chatting amiably with her about the beautiful bright yellow winter jasmine climbing across the walls of her garden.

Soon we were out again onto the Holloway Road, dodging cars and buses, and mingling with crazy throngs of shoppers as we hopped from pub to pub, our talk becoming more bizarre at each place until the orange glow of evening took hold and the shoppers on the street became drunks like us. After numerous pubs, Neil was able to finagle us into another party, this time in Hackney.

Almost every night and every day passed this way in the new period of my life where the morose brooding behind my mother's curtains suddenly gave way to a riotous drunken haze of colour and noise. If I felt any regret it was only because my novel was unwritten on my laptop and by the time I woke up each afternoon it was time to go out again. However, there was a slight, lingering feeling of being a hanger-on. At the parties we went to I knew nobody, and usually Neil didn't either. Yet soon he was virtually playing host, while I was merely being suffered as a necessary side-effect of Neil's irrepressible presence. I tried to introduce him to some of my friends, but he quickly tired of them while they just thought he was mad, and we left early from whatever gathering we had ruined.

As for Neil, he said he had no friends. Since leaving Feltham Young Offenders Institution he had drifted from town to town, making deep and intimate but not lasting connections. He had more phone numbers than his mobile's memory could handle, but each of them was accompanied by a long and extravagant story about why he couldn't call because he owed the person money or a favour or had slept with his wife or stolen his car. So we sloped around north London from pub to pub and invited ourselves to parties with strangers.

Then, one day, Neil was gone. For several weeks I heard nothing until, just before Christmas, a battered postcard smudged with rain informed me that Cornwall in December was a truly beautiful place, full of crags and rocks, and monuments to people and gods nobody can remember anymore. He was staying in a friend's old cottage working his way quickly through a dusty old Cornish dictionary, he told me, as if he were remembering the ancient words rather than having to learn them anew. He had got as far as 'gwreg' ('wife'), but couldn't find anyone to teach him the correct pronunciations. So he was fumbling through, making up his own sounds and planning to get all the way through to z by New Year. He signed off 'Dha weles' without even putting his name.

Though who else could it be? The friends with whom I now spent my time, the collection of failed writers and 'mature students' who only a few weeks ago had been in my naïve young eyes the height of wit, erudition and wisdom, seemed like shades. None of them could have composed something so spontaneous and true as that smudged, creased old postcard. Its spidery black script streaked across the page, winding its way between the lines of the address and spilling over onto the bright yellow sands and blue sea on the other side. I was gripped by it and wanted to jump into my old blue-green Nissan Figaro and burn down the M4 to spend Christmas with Neil, learning Cornish and drinking whisky in the rickety old fisherman's cottage with the fire crackling and the treacherous winds lashing the windowpanes. But I lacked the heart for it. Instead I toasted Christmas with sherry in my mother's living room with relatives who always made me feel dead.

New Year's Eve came around and I was feeling as lonely as the grave. I had been invited to a couple of parties but knew exactly what they would be like and had no interest in going. I fully intended to see the New Year in with my mother, using my desire for solitude as a pretext to be a good son for once and help her through what my vapid relatives had sententiously predicted would be a 'difficult time' for her. By ten o'clock, however, the canned laughter from the television was making me suicidal and I knew that my mother could see it because she offered to turn it off. I hastily declined and she looked relieved as I sped out of the door and into the cold dark night that was full of animal yelps and whoops.

I pulled the top down on my Figaro so I could hear all the roistering and perhaps let some of it rub off on my lonely soul. I drove down Hornsey Road into the madness of Holloway. But it did nothing for me. After driving up and down for some time, I parked in a side street and did something truly absurd. I went to Donna's Kebabs, ordered an extra large kebab with hot sauce and chomped down on it, watching the clock tick down to midnight. All the time I fully expected Neil to come crashing in, full of ideas and enthusiasm, dragging me out of my solitude into some pulsating pit of desperate young drinkers trying to live just a little more before the end of the year.

Of course, nothing happened. Neil was buried in his Cornish dictionary, probably halfway through 'y', feverishly fighting his way to the end, and I was left with myself. It was another slow night for Donna's Kebabs — everyone with anywhere to go was somewhere else. Around midnight, the spotty young man who had been left in charge shuffled out from behind the counter with two cans of beer and set one before me, saying, 'Don't tell anyone, yeah?'

Midnight came and went. We clinked cans. For the kebab boy, the fear of getting caught seemed to outweigh the pleasure of rebelling against Donna, and he looked constantly out of the window for the police, hardly talking to me. About ten minutes later, with his can still half-full, he went back behind the counter. I was bad company anyway and, to avoid getting Donna's Kebabs closed down over the worst, smallest, most dismal and depressing New Year's party in history, I took my beer out into the street. People were cheering as they swayed past in flush-cheeked groups, arms around each other, and several tried to gather me up and carry me along in their tide of celebration, but I resisted and broke free. Everything felt wrong, and all I could think about was that one more year had passed with my great literary novel still unwritten. I had wasted too many nights on the Holloway Road and too many mornings lying in bed too sick and confused to do anything. My laptop brimmed with half-finished thoughts. Abandoned chapters littered the dark corners of its hard drive. It was taking longer and longer to start up in the mornings, evidence, the shop said, of a virus, but to me a symptom of the weight of hackneyed, cliché-ridden prose clogging its arteries. The more I wrote, the slower it ran, as if in protest at the poverty of my writing.

A few days later, in a grand New Year experiment, I tried taking a notebook to a café and writing there, as I had on long dreamy university days, but the process now felt foreign. My hand ached quickly, the dull characters in the café distracted me too easily, and writing even the simplest sentence seemed to require far too much effort. I realised that I could never have churned out so many megabytes of dross had I been forced to write longhand, or even to feed paper through an old-fashioned typewriter. At some point my body would have rebelled against the wasted effort, as it rebelled now in those cafés at every trite sentence that my tired brain formed. I went back to my room and let my fingers glide swiftly over the keys. Better to produce garbage than to produce nothing at all, the writing books always said. So for two months I cluttered my hard drive with more megabytes of ponderous, inelegant prose, all the while feeling like more of a fool.

So when Neil came racing into my mother's house one bright March morning, I embraced him as my saviour. He did look curiously messianic, standing there in the hallway with the bright orange sun flooding in through the open door at his back. It made him almost glow around the edges as his bright brown eyes shone childlike and his thick face smiled broadly but serenely at me. He looked at once like a man who had discovered some important secret and like a child eager to discover a new one. Probably all this was in my head, a product of the months of despair and their sudden end in a blaze of glorious spring light. We hugged like old brothers, and my mother stood watching us in bemusement. She liked Neil for his polite talk of winter jasmine and for the simplicity and kindness that lay beneath all that loud masculine youth, laughter and energy, but she could sense that he was dangerous too. She knew he would leave again soon but that this time I would go with him, and she warned me before I left not to follow him everywhere he went.

'Keep your own mind, Jack,' she said. 'Don't let yourself be led anywhere you don't want to go.'

I kissed her and said I'd be fine, and indeed at that time I felt stronger and more independent than at any time in my life; the idea of going anywhere I didn't want to was ridiculous and slightly hurtful. By that time Neil and I had spent a week or two exploring every pub, bar, club and kebab shop, curry house, chicken shack and burger joint on the Holloway Road, and were thoroughly sick of London and all its grey grimy misery. We'd even taken to trying the pubs around my mother's house in sedate little Crouch End, disturbing the faithful old dogs at the feet of the old men with their crossword in one hand, pipe in the other and their pint of bitter half-drunk on the table in front of them.

We decided to cause some havoc to shake them out of their dead filmy-eyed smiling expressions and get them to put down their pipes and papers and express something, if only anger. But the first place we tried it, a tiny little place with net curtains on the window, a crackling fire and a leafy beer garden out back, nobody rose to the bait. We cursed loudly, danced and shouted and even took a swig of one old man's beer. But nobody said a word. The barman stared at us with an ambiguous expression on his face, and the customers just buried themselves in their crosswords, waiting for us to go away and leave them alone. We soon did, feeling so ashamed of the whole thing that we bought a round of beers for everyone before we left.

After that we got a bottle of whisky from an off-licence on Hornsey Road and went down the hill to dark dirty old Elthorne Park to sit among the sad old winos, to drink and smoke. Neither of us said very much, not even Neil, who usually only seemed to stop speaking to eat, sleep or kiss someone. I don't know what he was thinking, but I was thinking of my father, who had worked all his life in a government office up in the city and travelled home on the same train every night, always stopping on his way back from the station for a quick pint and a chat with his friends before coming home to dinner. I imagined how he would have looked at Neil and me if we'd interrupted his quiet pint one tired evening with foolish attempts to goad him, how he would have told the story later over dinner with a sad shake of his head.

'We must leave tomorrow,' Neil said into the night. A couple of winos looked over; we'd been silent so long that they must have forgotten we were there.

2

The next morning we packed all our things into my little blue-green Figaro, waved goodbye to my mother and weaved through back streets clogged with parked cars and school children. Finally we reached the big bustling A1, snorting with buses, taxis and commuters. The little Figaro eased its way through a gap in the solid London-bound traffic and nosed over to the right, heading up the broad main road towards the holy parks and magical castles of Edinburgh. We put the top down, even though it was a grey, cold March morning, and Neil stood up and yelled at the commuters to turn around and head north.

'You're free! You're free!' he kept shouting, but all he got for his trouble were a few shy smiles and a stern ticking off from a policeman who flagged us down in Hendon. He was about to give Neil a lot more than a ticking off until his radio crackled and he got called away to something more important than a couple of over-exuberant young men in a poncey old car. As the blue lights flashed off up the street, Neil laughed a dry laugh and said, 'Tosser. C'mon, let's get going again.'

I pulled out and headed north, but the altercation had created an embarrassing fluttering in my chest as my heart briefly took on a funky syncopated jazz rhythm. I pulled over at a dreary parade of shops and said I wanted to get a cup of coffee for the road. Neil didn't want anything and he stayed in the car as I walked uncertainly to the smoky little café with fogged-up windows. I bought a coffee that I didn't really want, watching fascinated as the girl behind the counter performed some complex operation with frothing milk, loud gurgling and huge clouds of steam, before dropping into the paper cup a spoonful of Sainsbury's instant coffee granules from a huge budget-sized tin.

I couldn't believe that such an innocent little conversation with a policeman could have left me so shaken. I bought a bottle of water, too, drank that and took my sad little cup of instant coffee back to the car, feeling ashamed. Neil held it for me as I drove, and fortunately he ended up drinking it too, all the while telling me in great detail about his first contact with the police at the age of thirteen and his great wide-eyed terror of those big black uniforms, their batons, helmets and radios.

Somewhere near Borehamwood, after a slow steady crawl towards the M25, he finally got tired of talking and, reaching shyly into the battered old leather bag at his feet, said in his deep dry voice, 'Got a surprise in here for you, mate.' He rummaged for a good few minutes in the small bag, muttering under his breath all the while, until with a flourish he produced a big square box. 'On the Road,' he said, slipping an old cassette into the player. 'I discovered this in Cornwall and listened to it right through from start to finish three or four times. That's how come I only got to 'k' in Cornish. I would've finished learning that beautiful ancient language if it hadn't been for this tape that kept me up all night listening to its sweet aching search for enlightenment in a big old drive all across America and back again, with parties, girls, drinks, cabooses, jalopies and Dean Moriarty balling the jack at every turn. Now all that talk about angels, locusts, lambs and crosses I could take it or leave it, but if you told me that this stuff was the word of God I might just believe you.'

He played it, and the slightly nasal young voice of Matt Dillon twanged out the famous opening sentences that I had read myself many years earlier; although I didn't want to tell Neil that because he was so excited with

21

his discovery and wanted desperately to share it with the closest friend of that particular time. Who was I to tell him that I had read it when I was thirteen and had fallen in love with it for a year or two, along with some of the other great American romantic classics, before abandoning them for the more subtle, nebulous attractions of Peter Nadas and Gao Xingjian? He would have been crushed, and I would have felt like a supercilious literary type who couldn't take anything seriously unless it had at least thirty pages of endnotes unravelling its convoluted and deliberately opaque intertextuality. So I smiled and listened along with Neil, amused to glance across and see him muttering the lines along with Matt Dillon, as if it were a psalm and he was a faithful worshipper obeying Kerouac's call to prayer.

The traffic slowed to walking pace, and up ahead blue lights flashed. The Figaro juddered, its engine restless. It had a tendency to heat up when it stayed still too long — it liked to feel the cooling air flowing through. I glanced at the dial, which seemed to be broken because it was slumped at the bottom indicating that the engine was stone cold. The line of cars was moving just enough to prevent me from turning the engine off, and I fretted and tried to listen to the sound of the engine over Matt Dillon rattling on about Carlo Marx and holy lightning.

The police cars were pushing traffic off the A1, which was closed up ahead, and onto the M25 — a long crawling grey stream of frustration beneath us. 'I don't believe it,' I said sullenly. 'All our plans to follow the same road all the way to Edinburgh just shot to shit because the police decided to close the road.'

Neil stared ahead placidly. 'It's alright, Jack,' he said. 'A1, M1, Z1, none of it's really important. When you think about it, this here diversion was in fact the most inevitable thing that could possibly have happened to us. The road is like life. How many times does life let you take a straight road all the way to where you're going? No, it has to throw up obstacles and diversions and make you go all around the back of beyond just to get a few yards further up the line.'

'Poor old Sal Paradise just wanted to go west, and here he is now standing up on big old Bear Mountain in the rain with no prospect of a ride. And sorry to spoil it for you old friend but soon he'll give up and get a ride back to New York where he started from, before heading west on an expensive interstate bus ride that eats up half the money he's saved for the trip. So really there's almost no point in planning anything out at all,

23

because life is so infinitely complex that you can almost never just take a straight road from A to B without going via the whole rest of the alphabet first, and all because a butterfly happened to flap its wings in Thailand.'

He chattered happily on in this vein, not bothering to turn off the tape, so that his words merged with those of Jack Kerouac, Sal Paradise and Matt Dillon, and the effort of trying to disentangle them distracted me from the misery I would normally have felt at the hopelessly clogged traffic, drivers honking impotently and forcing their way urgently from one blocked lane to the next.

Nevertheless, it was impossible to avoid being touched by the sad lonely need with which Neil poured his heart and soul into living out Sal Paradise's ancient quest, utterly oblivious to the fact that while Sal had hitched a ride on some farmer's old jalopy that was now halfway across the Great Plains, our old jalopy was stuck in traffic on the outskirts of Potter's Bar, on the wrong road and heading very slowly in the wrong direction. And, furthermore, it wasn't even a real old jalopy, but a modern hatchback made to look old by some clever marketing executives in Japan.

At the next service station I pulled off.

'There's no point,' I said. 'We might as well sit here instead of out there.'

Neil agreed happily, and the Figaro found itself a spot in the middle of a colossal sprawl of asphalt under grey skies that were starting to spit rain. In the comforting neon of the service station we ate junk food and watched the nervous salesmen in white shirts and red ties making loud calls on their mobiles, the bad-tempered families taking refuge, as we were, from the traffic outside, old couples cheerfully drinking tea, the only people with nowhere to go in a hurry. We made up lives for them and when that got boring Neil stood up abruptly and went over to a young suited man who was talking particularly aggressively into his phone about meetings and sales targets. He leaned over his shoulder and, mimicking a female voice, said, 'Come back to bed, big boy. I want you so bad it hurts.'

The poor man covered his phone too late, grabbed his bag and ran away from Neil, pouring pleading explanations into the phone as he went. That kept us entertained for a time, but Neil, I now became aware, was like a child who tires quickly of every diversion. In the drunken, loud mobs of life in the pubs of Holloway Road I had never really noticed it, but sitting there in the sober neon glare of morning, with my brain tired and sluggish, and nothing but the inside of a service station to look at, I felt Neil to be a vortex voraciously sucking life out of those around him and still constantly needing more.

In desperation I proposed video games, and he jumped up, raced across the hall and had deposited his pound coin in the slot before I was even halfway there. I slid my coin in, too, but it was a car racing game and I was far behind. Still, he generously slowed down to let me catch up, and just as I was overtaking him he turned his wheel and slammed his car into mine, whooping and laughing as my imaginary car hurtled off into an imaginary stand full of spectators. I cut across the grass and was back on the track just behind him, and we gleefully fought it out lap after lap, sinking our coins into the machine to keep it going for another couple of minutes, not caring that in our zeal to fight each other we were constantly losing the race. Ten more minutes, though, and Neil was bored with this, too, and so was I, for I was itching to get out into a real car again, even if it was slower, older and more ponderous than the flashy sports cars that danced and weaved across the screen, and even if the traffic was still a solid sticky mass on the vast motorway somewhere outside this windowless world of lights and emptiness.

The road was not on Neil's mind, however. 'Look at those girls over there,' he said, nudging me. 'Let's go wherever they're going.'

I looked over. They were a gaggle of giggling girls, barely old enough to be out of school. They saw us staring and sent a screeching volley of giggles echoing up into the heights of the vast rain-smeared perspex roof far above.

Neil walked over with the swagger of a gunman in a saloon, took the tallest, blondest one lightly by the arm and whispered to her, 'Do you believe in love at first sight?'

She giggled, looked back at her friends and finally shook her head.

'I know, neither did I,' said Neil in an urgent whisper. 'I thought it was a bunch of romantic crap designed to sell bad books and boring films. But then I saw you and all that changed. I've seen the light. Felt the thunder clap, seen the lightning-bolt flash before my eyes. It's a beautiful thing.'

The look in his face was beatific, and I swear he had tears in his eyes. If he wasn't chatting up young girls in service stations, he could have had a successful career as an extra in a televangelist's show.

The girl seemed to buy it, too, for she was soon telling him her name, which I have long since forgotten, and that the four of them were heading for Wales on their Easter holidays, from school or college I could never tell, but I was glad to know that at least one of them was old enough to drive. Neil casually invited himself along and was gesturing to me too. The girls appraised me like a ragged dress in a second-hand charity shop sale. I couldn't stand it and told them to go along without me.

'Aw, come on, Jack, it'll be fun,' Neil said pleadingly, and I admit I did look at the three remaining girls for a few seconds, but they looked back at me with such distaste that I muttered a curt, 'It's fine.'

'Come on, we'll come back for the Figaro later,' he said in a high-pitched wheedling voice.

'I'm not leaving my car at some service station.'

'Well then, you can follow us.'

'I'm not following anybody,' I said, and walked off, giggles ringing in my ears.

The rain was coming down hard as I stalked back across the car park. The Figaro has never coped well with rain: its roof retracts easily in sunshine but never quite snaps back into place firmly, leaving thin cracks into which rainwater irresistibly insinuates itself. The water then trickles slowly down the insides, pools on the floor and steams up the windows. When I got in, I could feel the damp already, as wet inside as out. I switched on the engine, and instantly the cassette whirred into life with the interminable saga of Sal Paradise speeding across some State or other.

I switched it off with a violence that surprised me, resolving that very minute to have nothing further to do with Mr Neil Blake, a man who betrays his friends for a lark in a car with a group of giggling schoolgirls. How could he expect me to abandon my car and go off to Wales with a group of strangers? I pulled out of my space angrily, drawing a timid peep of the horn from an old man who was trying to pass and had to swerve to avoid me. I didn't care. I drove through the lines of parked cars at reckless speed, accelerating all the way back to the motorway, where the cars were now starting to crawl again.

I crawled with them for a while and then swerved off at the next junction to fiddle my way through quaint old St. Albans and up to the A5, deliciously straight on the map but, as it turned out, so clogged with cars and lorries that I couldn't reach top gear. Around Milton Keynes the traffic thinned, the cars sped up, and my mood started to lighten again. Neil

Blake was not my only friend in the world. I would head up to York to see my old university mate Oscar, writer of romances for women of a certain age. I envied his success with a passion as violent as my contempt for his novels, which were of the kind that I believe will soon be produced automatically by computers. Nevertheless, I always did my best to hide this from him, and we had a good time when we concentrated on drunken remembrances of times past. I had planned to stop off there on our way north, introduce him to my new friend Neil and have a great old time. Well, I decided, I would do the same without Neil.

I fumbled for the radio, found a decent tune and turned it up high as the green hills rolled past and I followed the straight old road north, feeling good about myself and finished with my friend. So straight, this road. Somewhere from the back of my mind I dredged up the knowledge that this used to be Watling Street, the old Roman road from Dover to Wroxeter, at that time a major city. I slowed down as I approached Towcester, an important staging point on the old road. It was a disappointment, of course. Even to imagine Roman legions at camp was impossible in this anonymous agglomeration of clothing chains, supermarkets and dark pubs. Only a few bored teenagers on bikes stared blankly at my Figaro as it purred through the town and out the other side in no more than a couple of minutes. Soon I was back on the main road, heading north again, and gunning the engine as much as my Figaro would allow. I became slowly hypnotised by the way the white centre line seemed to roll out from the side of my right wheel for mile after mile after straight, monotonous mile.

The rain had stopped now and I put the windows down, letting fresh country air flood me and clear my head of Neil, his foolish talk and his childish needs. I ejected his tape and tossed it onto the back seat, where I noticed all his luggage piled up in a big ungainly heap. I tapped the brakes momentarily, absurdly thinking of going back to the service station to give him his bags, but then I pressed firmly on the accelerator and jumped forward, ever further north. Neil had four young girls to attend to him, so what need had he of luggage?

Still, the sight of the bags in my rear-view mirror irritated me. I had rid myself of Neil, Jack Kerouac and the tiresome pointless travels and travails of Sal Paradise. I was immersed in the calm, quiet solitude of a long journey on an open road. I had time and space to think without another person thinking for me. I had freedom to do what I wanted without being told. Yet his bags were still there, a battered old brown leather suitcase and a ragged cloth bag stuffed full of crumpled clothes that spilled out of the burst seams. Their shambling impracticality mocked my straight-laced, neat little wheeled suitcase on the seat beside them.

I kept my foot pressed down. The Figaro roared its protest, but complied. With speed, Neil faded from my mind again. Even the fields, cows and occasional houses on either side faded into an impressionistic blur, and all that remained was the shuddering wheel I gripped and the solid, unwavering white line peeling out in front of me for mile after mile after mile, widening occasionally to accommodate a right turn but bending inexorably back into alignment with the front of my Figaro. I thought of the Joads heading west, of Sal Paradise hitching rides across America and back again, even of poor perverted old Humbert Humbert drifting from State to State with his beloved Lo chewing bubble gum at his side. I thought, then, that I understood some of what Neil was saying about the mystique of the road. It truly didn't matter that I was on the A5 instead of the A1. The feeling of swift progress, even in the wrong direction, is an immensely powerful one, and speeding past Astcote in an old blue-green Figaro exhilarated me.

Flash! My stomach lurched, and my foot impotently stabbed at the brake. Sixty pounds and three points on my licence, in an instant. All automatic, impersonal. I raged at the injustice of it, and slowed to a steady sixty as my blood raced in torrents through my body. The camera had been placed just past the brow of a hill and was partially obscured by a tree, so that even if I had been paying more attention I would have struggled to see it in time to slow down. There wasn't even a policeman I could plead with or lie to, before having to grudgingly accept that I was in the wrong. Just a flash of a camera and an automatic penalty that I couldn't fight except by going to court, and that would be pointless due to the evidence; there was something dishonest about it. I remembered Neil yelling at me in one of our long rambling bar conversations on the Holloway Road: 'It's all about power,' he'd said. 'They trot out all these casualty statistics and tell you it's all for your own good, but really it's about letting you know they are watching you and can fuck with you any time they want.' And, as we came out of the pub, he'd yelled abuse at a CCTV camera on the corner, drawing quite a crowd, to his delight.

I rolled on sourly, the peace and happiness gone. The road lost its mystique and became something to be endured, just half a day of tarmac tedium separating me from York. Soon I was yawning and pulled into a roadside café for a cup of watery tea and a tough gristly old sausage in spongy bread. A trucker stood smoking a cigarette and blowing clouds of steam from the top of his tea. I raised my eyebrows in greeting, and he looked away to the fields. I walked back to the car, tossing the dried-up remains of my sausage in the bin.

I got a few clear miles done before slowing through the outskirts of Rugby, and I took the opportunity of the dawdling traffic to balance the atlas on my knees and discover that the A5 was veering too far west and I would need to turn off. I jagged back east through the anonymous, slow-moving streets of Leicester, and veered north-east on the A46, until at Newark-on-Trent I met up again with the great A1 that I had left behind so long ago. Soon the road widened and the traffic slackened, and I pressed forward, ever further north. With speed and a fixed destination, all the tortured memories and furious imagined confrontations with official-dom slowly faded away into the blur of the passing fields. For an hour or two, as I drove through the weakening afternoon light, all that mattered was the road. I willed the Figaro forward as fast as it would go without breaking the speed limit, always going due north, leaving London and Neil and the speeding fine far, far behind. So intent was I on heading north that I missed the turning completely, and had to swing round onto minor roads and cut across high, open country all the way back to York.

Up there on the moors you can get a sense of the wild England that existed before Boots and Sainsbury's and Toys 'r' Us. You can picture shepherds, nomads and horse-riders following ancient tracks through the mist and mud to God-knows-where. You can see old dusty careworn tribes killing and dying for causes that time would swiftly make irrelevant. The heather-coated hillsides seem to be the custodians of these memories, keeping the old tribesmen alive as if the Roman legions had never marched down Watling Street, killed them with ease, and renamed their towns and gods. Towcester doesn't seem to exist up there, its bored teenagers and vacant shoppers seeming to belong to a different time and place. This landscape is empty and lonely and, unusually for England, spacious. It's a landscape of possibilities, where for a while you feel as if you can breathe air that hasn't recently passed through someone else's lungs. Then the road dips down into the suburbs, and you find yourself waiting at a red light by an off-licence as tired men shuffle past and cars flash across the junction in front of you on meaningless errands to nowhere. You're back in the conqueror's territory, the old camp of Eboracum, where the tribesmen whose presence you felt up on the lonely hillsides don't dare to venture for fear of crucifixion. You might even swing your car around, as I did, and head back into the hills, but you won't find what you're looking for. Those feelings come quickly and pass forever.

You could spend a lifetime driving across the Yorkshire moors and never see anything more than acres of swaying grass. Or that fleeting glimpse of something unfathomably big might come to you at a completely different time, when you're at home in bed, or on a train through the suburbs, or waiting for a bus. And the absolutely certain thing is that you will never understand it or even be able to explain it to anyone else, except in the vague, confused way that I am doing now. And you will go back to the same suburb where the same tired men shuffle past and the same cars buzz around, going nowhere, and you will forget about the ancient tribesmen, or the angels or gods or the clouds or the big black void or whatever it was you thought you saw or imagined, and you will tell yourself it was all in your head. Soon you will be firmly among the living again, and it will be as if you are dead.

If you are particularly foolish, you will become one of those writers or artists who spends their whole career trying to describe or recapture that fleeting glimpse, which everyone gets once but only once, and like Shakespeare and Van Gogh and Schiele and Steinbeck and Nadas and Hendrix and Borges and Soyinka and Cervantes, you will fail to describe anything but a small individual corner of the vast reality you thought you saw. All your work will be a pale shadow of what you know to be possible, and when you realise it you will either wish yourself a shopping drone like the people who shuffle around you or, like Hemingway, you will kill yourself.

3

When I got to Oscar's house, I felt sick. It was a beautiful elegant old Georgian townhouse, and I knew that he owned it outright. There are a lot of women in England who will buy every single romance novel you write, even if they are all the same. And I knew for a fact that Oscar churned out two a year like clockwork, getting up at dawn and writing for three hours, producing an even three thousand words and then spending the rest of his day in quiet contemplation of the Times crossword or buried in some historical book that he would use to give his next novel a gloss of realism that his readers would love, enabling them not only to enjoy a vapid romance but to feel that they were learning something of seventeenth-century Florence or nineteenth-century London in the process.

Three thousand words a day, every day of the week. Before I had stumbled downstairs to my mother's tea and toast, Oscar had produced more words than I would in three months of tortured wrestling with my perpetually half-written novel. Three thousand words a day, fifteen thousand words a week, sixty thousand words a month. In three months, presto! you have a suitably thick five hundred leaf page-turner to fill a Christmas stocking or holiday suitcase. The next two months are spent on revisions, he'd told me once, and after that he has a month off to 'recharge his batteries' in time for the next novel. 'Recharge your batteries', I had observed, is a hideous cliché, which he'd seemed to take as a dig at his cliché-ridden romances and replied that clichés only become clichés because they are a really good way of expressing an idea. Being popular doesn't make something bad, he'd said, any more than being unpopular makes something good, which I took as a dig at my own unpublished, unwanted work (even my short stories have mustered nothing more than a stack of rejection slips). And we hadn't spoken since that day, a couple of years earlier.

Now that I stood outside the imposing railed staircase of his townhouse, I felt an urge to turn around and drive back to London. I could be there by late evening, just in time to get my mother to make me a toasted sandwich before bed. The prospect comforted my soul as it stood naked and hurting on this grey cold northern street with the wind whipping it, and the remembered anger and humiliation eating away at it from the inside. Suddenly I saw a small white paper flapping on the door. As I got closer I could make out the words: 'In the King's Arms. See you there.'

I felt embarrassed, and slightly sad. At one time that note would have been left for me. We would routinely skip lectures and go to one pub or another around Oxford, drinking the afternoons away in a dark smoky haze of cheap ale and bar billiards. Other friends would come and go, but we were the unchanging core, always comfortable in each other's company, assuming that the friendship would last forever. But now jealousy stung my eyes in the sharp north wind, as I saw a note left for a new drinking companion. Oscar had no idea I was arriving: the visit was meant to be a surprise. Now I was stuck in the cold grey afternoon, with the faint haze of sun behind the clouds sinking ever lower, abandoned by my new friend for some schoolgirls and by my old friend for a newer friend.

My only option was to turn my car around and barrel it all the way down the motorway to dreary London and my mother's house to face her polite equivocation at my latest failure. Her son, to whom she had given the best education, whom she had loved and doted on and taught and trained to be the best he could be in the world, her son who had passed every exam he ever took and graduated with honours from the best university in the country, before failing to hold down a job for longer than a few months and finally retreating home to write failed novels from behind his mother's skirts, her wonderful failure of a son had now failed even to take a simple road trip. He would return as he always returned to his poor loving mother, to hear her kind words and drink her comforting tea and feel safe and warm again; and she would oblige as she always obliged, but surely somewhere under-neath her cheery words, comfort and love, disappointment festered? Not even Jesus Christ himself could be so forbearing. The thought of disappointing her gnawed at me with each new failure, making her loving words ring false and her sweet tea taste sour and watery. I found myself sometimes even despising her for her failure to despise me, and for this I despised myself more.

To avoid all this confusion and disorder, I did not turn my car around and head south to the warmth, but walked off into the cold darkening afternoon in search of the King's Arms. In this respect I did still know Oscar. He still didn't like to go too far for his pubs.

The King's Arms stood on the corner of his street exactly where I knew it would be, and it was exactly the kind of pub I knew it would be, too. It was not a modern, refurbished pub of the kind you'd find on the Holloway Road, all bright lights, loud music and high ceilings from which shouted conversations would bounce dizzyingly, but neither was it a rough old spit-and-sawdust place where the beer was laced with danger and simply allowing your eyes to stray in the wrong direction could bring an eye-bulging, vein-popping 'Wotchulookinatyoucunt?' It was a solidly old pub with a solidly middle-class clientele, a friendly middle-aged barman, a good range of real ales, ivy climbing the old brick walls and the original hardwood floor sanded and polished to a fashionable sheen. I knew all this about it and more as soon as I saw it rising up out of the gloomy afternoon.

At first I couldn't see Oscar through the haze of pipe smoke and the men in thick jumpers crowding the bar, but then I spied the familiar curly brown hair spiralling up from a thin angular pale face buried in a pint of brown ale at a corner table, and I pushed my way politely through to him.

'Where's your friend?' I said.

'Jack!' he said. 'What kept you?'

'Well . . . ' I sputtered, not quite knowing

how to take this. It had been a while since I had visited, but then we had not parted on the best of terms, and he had not visited me either. Yet his face was open and smiling, and I was busy trying to consider what he could have meant, and found myself caught between a dozen different answers, able to commit to none.

'Jack!' came a deep booming voice from behind me. 'What kept you? Now I was just saying to your friend Oscar here that you are the most cautious driver I have ever come across, always fretful and afraid as if you think your little Nissan Figaro is a big bucking stallion that will get away from you if you don't keep it on the tightest of tight reins. And he was telling me about a certain time in your youth when you took an old Mini Metro onto a straight-as-a-die road and gunned it up to a hundred. I didn't believe a Metro could *do* a hundred, I mean physically do a hundred, and so I'm glad to see you here, Jack, to resolve this important and all-encompassing question once and for all beyond any doubt, so help me God.'

It was Neil, of course. He was clapping me on my back and punching me on my arm while he chattered on, I gaped and Oscar watched in silent amusement from behind his half-empty beer-frothed pint-glass. I sat down, bewildered, while Neil kept talking about all the things that he and Oscar had been talking about, urgently wanting to fill me in on every last detail of what had happened in his life, but omitting the very thing I wanted to know.

'How the fuck did you get here, Neil?'

Neil stroked his jaw. 'Ah yes, yes, now that is something very interesting to relate. Well, those girls, you see, turned out to be rather disappointing in their inherent conservatism, which of course is stamped onto their souls from an early age by parents, school, police, brownies, government, TV and all the other means of social control against which an individual is truly powerless and so of course I can't really blame them. But I was disappointed not to be able to undertake a truly harmless and exciting adventure with them, simply because one of them harboured some deep-seated fear that I was a serial killer or axe murderer or rapist or some such nonsense, and she communicated her sad sorry little fears to the rest of them like the commonest of common colds, and so our little trip was stillborn and I was left kicking my heels in a service station. I went looking for you, Jack, but of course you'd gone off already on your offended way leaving nothing but some tyre tracks on the wet greasy tarmac. I was truly at a loss until my hand hit a crumpled bit of paper in my pocket with your phone number on it, your home phone number that is, of course, because as we know you are firmly resistant to mobile phones and all they entail, characterise and symbolise about modern society and its tragic flaws. So I called it and your dear sweet mother answered, and I said we had become separated and she sounded so sad, poor thing, that I almost said it was a mistake and pretended to have seen you again, but then I didn't have the heart to do that either so I just hung limply on the end of the line while she fished around in her piles of papers for some contact details you'd left her for a friend you were planning to visit in York. I must say I was touched, Jack, by the idea of you giving your dear sweet mother some details of where you planned to go on your spontaneous road trip across Britain, just in case she needed to get in touch with you for anything, and I'm very grateful that you did because that's how I came to be here sitting in this pub with your delightful friend Oscar talking about life and the world and your place in it, having taken a bus back to London and from there taken the National Express coach service, a very cheap option I might add, all the way up the motorway to York in just a few short hours, while you probably meandered your way across back roads, admiring hedgerows and churches and sheep in fields along the way and stopping all the time for cups of tea, so that I got here before you and came straight out to this here pub to drink some excellent beer and have a good time getting to know your friend. Speaking of beer, you appear to have your hands empty there, my friend.'

'Yes, I was just going to . . . '

'Oh, that's very kind of you, very kind indeed. Mine's a Guinness.'

'Old Speckled Hen,' Oscar said from the corner, downing the frothy brown remains in his glass in one loud gulp.

And I wandered off to the bar to buy three overpriced pints, wondering all the while exactly what I would say when I got back, if indeed I had a chance to say anything at all before a torrent of words started flooding over me again. I looked back to the table and saw Neil and Oscar laughing together, and didn't know what to think. I had wanted this, and yet now I found myself worrying that both would find each other more interesting than they found me, and that I would end up on the sidelines of my own friendships. And as the afternoon turned to evening and the beer flowed over the scarred wooden table, I found my fears growing. On a table with two writers, Neil was the one with all the stories to tell, and I noticed he was directing them more to Oscar than to me. Then, when Oscar opened his ponderous mouth to make some obvious observation, Neil nodded his head vigorously, his beer slopping in his glass in his enthusiasm. He even professed a sincere interest in Oscar's writing, saying that romances are the most essential thing in the world to write about, for what is life but one big romance, full of longing and loving and secret desires?

And I sat watching this spectacle, drinking the beer as fast as I possibly could but always staying a round or two behind Neil and Oscar. I tried to interest them in going to a new bar, or to get some food, but they said they were happy where they were with their beer and the excellent hot chips from the bar, which Neil slathered in mayonnaise, a habit he'd picked up from some Norwegian girl he'd spent a riotous passionate summer with when he was, he said, barely old enough to understand the things she said she wanted to do with him, let alone do them. Of course this led into yet another long winding yarn, which Oscar followed assiduously, all the while gobbling the steaming chips and saying he would never use ketchup or brown sauce again.

The air, when we finally stepped outside, was chill and damp, slapping us awake from the fug of the pub, and we stood for a while on the corner of the street gazing up into the clear black sky, with the stars that we hadn't seen all the long dark winter in smoky London shrouded in a grey-orange impenetrable glow. I began howling at the big bright moon and Neil joined in louder and shriller, but Oscar soon shushed us, explaining in an urgent loud whisper that he lived around here and so on and so forth. So we stopped our howling and set off down some darkened side street of cold high brick buildings looking for something.

Soon Neil found what he was looking for. 'A kebab van,' he cried, and sprinted forward like a child answering the call to ice cream. Oscar smiled at me, shrugged and lumbered along behind, but I couldn't bring myself to rush. My stomach was bloated from all the beer poured down my gullet at breakneck speed for the last six hours or so, and the thought of piling a greasy kebab on top of all that sloshing frothing sourish liquid made me nauseous.

'Come on, Jack!' Neil shouted. 'I'm buying!'

'I'll pass,' I shouted. 'Don't feel so good.'

Neil looked at me, spoke a word or two to the kebab man and ran back, ushering me into a dark damp little alley between two old brick factories or warehouses or something, where he turned me roughly around and I thought for a panicked moment he was going to slash my throat, until I felt his body pressed up against my back and his thick hands gripping me just below the ribs. With one hard jerk inward and upward he sent all the beer and chips roaring up my throat and splattering out onto the damp dark bricks.

'Better out than in,' he said in a cheery voice, slapped me hard on the back, and walked on into the night, leaving me standing stooped like an old man over the acrid hot pool beginning to steam in the cold night air. When I got back to the kebab van, Neil handed me a large doner with extra hot sauce, and for a second I felt I would be sick again, but then a huge aching hunger ate me up from the inside and I grabbed at the kebab and tore into it as if it were my last supper.

'Ah, yes, there you are, my friend,' Neil said between mouthfuls. 'As I suspected, you are now fully cured and ready for some more action, whereas if you had continued to fight against the course of nature and the currents of the universe, you would have been sick and miserable until some time tomorrow morning. Now we can go to find a club, yes?'

Oscar, however, said that he had to get up early in the morning to write, and wouldn't budge even in the face of Neil's most expert and manipulative wheedling and cajoling. 'York's crap for clubs anyway,' he insisted. 'A bunch of spotty pubescent boys trying to grope underage, underdressed girls in a dark, sweaty pit, with mindless pop music jangling away too loud for anyone to hear anything.'

'Sounds like the clubs in London,' I said drolly.

'Precisely, my friend, only perhaps with a slightly younger clientele, and that is precisely why we must go right away, because we have the advantage of a few years of experience, good looks and a lack of spots, and will sweep those poor unsuspecting girls off their underdressed feet and will have the time of our lives with them.'

Oscar didn't see at all. He pointed us grudgingly in the direction of what he called the least bad club in town, gave me a spare key with strict instructions not to wake him when we got home, and stomped off into the night, steaming streams of breath flowing over the right shoulder of his thin, vanishing little silhouette, which paid no heed whatsoever to Neil's attempts to call him back.

'Well, what does he know, eh, Jack?' he said. 'Let him go home and write his romances, and we'll make our romances right here with some sweet underdressed Yorkshire girls in a dark sweaty pit. Right? Right?' And off he walked, his head bent to the sharpening breeze, and I stood for a moment choosing who to follow, before stepping off after Neil.

Now I must say that I have never been a big clubber. Even when I have been stoked up on ecstasy, running on speed or dizzily oblivious from some good marijuana, I have found nothing in nightclubs to hold my attention. I also resent being made to queue like a naughty schoolboy outside the head-master's office while a thick-necked bouncer in a tight black t-shirt appraises me. And I laugh inwardly at my fellow clubbers, grown men and women reduced to snivelling self-conscious children, desperately wondering if their clothes are cool enough to pass the scrutiny of the meathead on the door, who, for a small period on a Saturday night, holds absolute power over them. By the time I have worked my way inside to pay the outrageous entrance fee and buy the one round of drinks I can afford for the rest of the night, I am usually so resentful that it would be impossible for me to enjoy myself even if I could dance.

The queue outside 'Manhattan', however, was mercifully short, and Neil made quick work of the bouncer, who seemed in any case to have little interest in us. Inside was just as Oscar had described, and instantly I felt an overwhelming tiredness flood my body, as the remembrance of the service station, the motorway, the roadside café, the Yorkshire moors, the police, the speed camera, the pub and the kebab van all flashed through my head at once. I felt as if I had been in this place before, and in a way I had, many times before. It was the same as dark, loud clubs all over the country, and the prospect of spending another few hours among the odour of sweat, flesh and cheap aftershave, buying overpriced drinks for women I could barely see and certainly couldn't hear, filled me with despondence.

As I was buying drinks at the bar, Neil had already made his way onto the dancefloor and was bouncing around with an abundance of energy but no rhythm. I took his beer to him, motioned that I was going to the toilet, took my own beer off to a dark corner and downed it quickly, watching Neil on the dancefloor circling wolf-like around a group of young girls. I couldn't bear to see the moment when he would strike, as the prospect both of his humiliation and of his success struck me as equally odious for reasons I could not quite describe. I slinked off to the toilets, urinated among a group of loud shouting youngsters overflowing with vodka, Red Bull and testosterone, and crept out into the night. As always at these times I felt old and out of place, wishing that, even if I couldn't write a novel or hold down a job, I was able to accomplish even the simplest things in life like having a good time.

The morning sun woke me early through the paper-thin curtains of Oscar's spare room. My head felt cloudy and my mouth was dry and rough. I got up and searched for Neil, but found only Oscar in the cosy living room hunched over his laptop, his fingers gliding easily over the keys in a soft, smooth torrent of words.

'Morning,' he said, without looking up from the screen or even stopping his soft tapping.

'Morning. Have you seen Neil?'

'No. Help yourself to cereal and stuff. Anything you can find in the kitchen is yours.'

'Thanks.' I started pottering around half-heartedly searching for something to eat while thinking of how Neil was probably in some student flat waking up with a young girl, Oscar was efficiently tapping out a new novel, and I was wandering around with a headache in a kitchen far from home looking for cereal I didn't want. I knew I had to get away from there, but to go where?

My big road trip depended for its success upon Neil Blake, for with all his betrayal and insensitivity, long winded stories, childish enthusiasm and infuriating lack of attention span, he was irrepressibly human and alive, and I craved his company as fervently as I craved solitude when I was with him. Driving and driving and driving all over Britain just didn't seem worthwhile without Neil chattering his incessant pseudo-philosophical life observations in the passenger seat.

Again I faced with horror the prospect of a long lonely drive home to my brave-faced mother, and I thought of my long half-finished novel sitting on my laptop and it seemed worthless junk, a mass of zeros and ones entered at great cost and being stored for no reason. My novel bore some relation to other books but none to life, and it swayed uncertainly between stubbornly esoteric intellectualism and slavish aping of the latest publishing fads, depending upon how desperate I was for publication at the time I happened to write each section. The result was an incoherent mess, self-righteous on one page and craven on the next. It needed massive revision, but first it needed to be finished, and how could I finish something so confused?

The front door slammed. I could hear Neil lurching down the hall, and I listened intently for the sound of an extra set of footsteps but could hear none.

'Are you ready, Jack?' he asked.

'Absolutely,' I replied.

'Then let's fire up that Figaro of yours and head off to the open road. I need to feel — '

'But what about Oscar? I mean, we've just arrived.'

'He has his readers, Jack,' he said, lowering his voice, but purely for effect because it was still loud enough for Oscar to hear from the other room. 'His readers are more important to him than his friends. You and I, Jack, we have no readers. We are free to live life as we want. We have no deadlines, no demands. Nobody is watching us. We could do anything or nothing at all.'

'I'll ask him,' I said, but really it was no more than the very kind of empty middle-class affectation of politeness that I was trying to escape from. The three of us knew that Oscar would stay to tap out romances on his laptop, and in any case the Figaro is essentially a two-seater car (there is a row of seats in the back, but anyone over four-foot-six has to sit with his knees around his ears), so to accommodate him would have required an extensive revision of our entire plans, something I had no real desire to do. And beyond that, something gnawed at me every time I was with him. The old college friendship had always been tinged with rivalry, but it had got worse over the years and now the rotting corpse of my jealous contempt for his work lay under the floor of all our conversations, inhibiting any genuine rekindling of our friendship.

So Neil and I bundled back into the Figaro, and Oscar got up from his laptop for long enough to wave us off at the door even though he was distracted all the time, probably thinking of those unwritten words mounting up by the minute as he stood there in the cold.

4

We headed due north on the old York Road, now a little-used byway so narrow in places that we had to squeeze right over to one side to let any rare oncoming cars slide past. There were faster alternatives, of course, but I wanted to travel on the old kind of road, the one that snakes right through the high streets of the ancient little market towns and villages, letting you gawp at the people shopping and talking, instead of being shuttled out to some bypass or ring road to fight it out with lorries and buses to get through a maze of traffic lights and mini-roundabouts.

This road jagged straight through the centre of little Sutton-on-the-Forest, Stillington, Marton Abbey and Brandsby. The sun glinted beautifully off the weathered grey stone, and I felt free again as York and all its noise and confusion faded to memory. I wondered what life must be like for these people in their small quiet towns with just a few shops and farms, the occasional pub or church, and a line of cottages strung like beads along the road. It was so far from everything I knew. I saw a 'For Sale' sign outside one cottage and wondered what the cost would be. Perhaps some fresh air, peace and light was what I needed to complete my great unfinished novel.

Neil was unusually quiet. I revelled in the silence for a while, but then it began to unnerve me. 'Beautiful, isn't it?' I said as we passed an old church steeple stretching up into the arching blue sky with a gently swaying black weathervane perched on top.

Neil smiled. 'Yeah, beautiful,' he said. 'Perhaps somewhere along the way we can stop at a little teashop with lace curtains on the windows and classical music on the stereo, and we can sip tea and eat scones off a little china plate with a fucking doily on it. Then we can take some photographs to add to our album with amusing little notes about the fun we had on our nice gentle little drive in the countryside. Then we can show them to our friends one evening over martini and nibbles.'

I puffed out my cheeks and tried to answer without sounding like a petulant child. 'Well, what do you want to do, then?'

'Ah, come on, Jack. I don't want to make you all upset and defensive. I just want to live a little bit before I die, that's all. And driving along some country road at forty-miles-an-hour looking at churches and cute little cottages is not living. It's dying, very slowly.'

'So what's living, Neil? Fucking school-girls? Drinking, smoking and taking drugs until you're too messed up to make sense of yourself or the world or anything in it? Talking shit all day long and acting as if it's some mystical truth handed down to you by God?'

Neil punched me so hard on the arm that the Figaro swerved across the road in alarm and almost clipped an old stone wall. '*That's* living, Jack!' he said in jubilation. 'Two friends telling each other the truth and getting angry and hateful at each other because they love each other so much. That's living! Gazing blankly at picture-postcard scenes and saying 'how nice' is not living. It doesn't teach us anything or cost us anything or make us feel anything, and so it is a slow steady march to the grave. Our little exchange of truths just now was worth more than all the driving, looking, drinking, smoking and womanising we could do in a lifetime.'

I looked ahead and thought about what he had said. 'I don't really see it,' I said finally. 'I don't feel any closer to any truths. I just feel as if my enjoyment of a drive in a beautiful part of the world has been ruined because it doesn't fit your particular idea of what living is. And this idea of living is something I don't really understand and I'm not sure that you do either.'

'Yes, yes,' Neil said thoughtfully, staring at a flock of birds crossing the clear blue sky. 'The lack of understanding is just the point. Do you think that if I understood the true meaning and definition of what life could and should be all about, I would be crammed into this little Figaro with you, lurching all over Britain in some kind of crazy medieval quest? I don't know, Jack. Nobody knows. The curse of our generation is that everything's been tried before. Drink, drugs, God, sex, meditation, masturbation, crystals, mush-rooms, peyote, shamanism, communism, consumerism, tai chi, feng shui, kung fu, flower power and TV shopping. It's obvious to anyone that our little road trip here is nothing more than a tired repetition of an age-old formula. But have you got any better ideas, Jack? Have you thought of something that nobody else in the world before you has thought of?'

I had eased off the accelerator so that I could hear this little speech, and the Figaro was cruising along quietly in third gear. I stared at the road ahead, unable to think clearly. 'Why can't we just have a good time? Drive along, chat, look at nice things? We don't have to answer the great questions that have plagued mankind since the dawn of time. It's just a road trip. Why does it have to be about meaning?'

Neil sighed, a long, deep, rasping sigh that seemed to issue from deep inside him and carry with it the weight of a thousand years' disappointment. Then he said, in an unusually quiet, soft, patient tone, as if addressing a slow child, 'Because, Jack, life is the search for meaning. I think, therefore I am. The unexamined life is not worth living. Basic wisdom, Jack, although Mr Aristotle really should have added that the unlived life is not worth examining either.'

'Socrates,' I said, but Neil didn't care for details like that. It was the obsession with details to the exclusion of truth that had made him despise school and turn to big, weighty books from which he could understand something, if not everything, of the bigger picture.

'It's about praxis, Jack,' he continued. 'I was reading about it just the other day. No thought without action, no action without thought. That's the problem. Too many people just acting without any thought at all, eating, shopping, working and dying without ever wondering what it was all about. That's not life, Jack. That's prolonged death, a long slow painful suicide from a poison that spread through the body the minute that person decided, some time early in life, to give up on fruitless dreaming and just be practical. And then the people who are examining life, the priests and philosophers and gurus, are not living it, so they can't possibly understand it either. So our quest, Jack, is to live and dream and examine at the same time. Thought and action — combined and inseparable. Praxis. It's hard to do, but the alternative is death.'

'I still don't know . . . '

Neil sighed again. 'Neither do I, Jack. I just get a glimpse every now and then, and then it's gone. And just now when we were arguing I got a glimpse, and it was more than I'd had so far this morning pottering around little villages in the sunshine like a couple of middle-aged tourists.'

'Fine,' I said. 'No more pottering.' And I slammed my foot down on the accelerator, making the Figaro jump down, roaring and juddering, into second gear, although with its little one-litre engine the speedometer barely moved.

'There you go, Jack! Let's see what she can do. You remember gunning your Mini Metro up to a hundred? *That* was living, Jack! Try it with your little Figaro here!'

I pressed my foot flat to the floor and the Figaro whined and screeched up past sixty,

sixty-five, seventy. The whole crate began to shake wildly, and a worrying cracking noise came from the roof, but I kept going.

'Wooooo!' Neil screamed. 'We have lift-off!'

Seventy-five, eighty, and still she held together. The road at this point was straight and smooth, although still narrow enough to cause me problems if anyone came in the other direction. But perhaps that was living, too. Perhaps you needed to risk death to be alive. I kept pressing hard, but then the road swooped up to the brow of a hill, and I remembered the sudden flash of the speed camera the other day and I eased my foot up. With the slope I didn't even have to brake. The needle dipped sharply down past eighty, seventy, sixty.

'What's going on?' Neil asked, and I explained the whole sad story of the speed trap, the sixty pounds and three penalty points.

'I can't afford to get caught again,' I said. 'Not two days in a row. I already have six points, so if they do me for yesterday I'll be up to nine. One more ticket after that and I'm banned. No more road trips. Not even a little cruise down the Holloway Road. I'd be banned for a year and would have to go to some remedial school for bad drivers where they'd teach me to be a good boy in the future.'

'What do they call it, the Ministry of Love?'

'Something like that. The point is, you don't want to fuck with them. You can't fuck with them. They've won already. The cameras are everywhere. There's nothing you can do about it. The days of balling the jack up to a hundred just to see how fast she can go are gone, Neil.'

We were silent for a while after that, the Figaro just cruising along at fifty. As it happens there was no camera over the brow of that particular hill, but not much further along I did see the familiar yellow box and the series of little white lines in the road, and I felt vindicated. Neil was sullen, but didn't seem to blame me. I could see he was fuming at the idea that the cameras and their shadowy owners had won a victory over him and was scheming his revenge. He didn't come up with anything, though. Nobody can.

Instead of heading up onto the North Yorkshire Moors as I'd planned, I swerved left onto the A170 to head back towards the A1, the original projected path up from the Holloway Road to Scotland. I still didn't really know what Neil wanted, but I was sad that I would not have another chance to see the big lonely moors further north, even bigger and lonelier than those I'd seen on the way to York. But somehow I doubted that I would see any ancient tribesmen again. The day was too bright and sunny, and with Neil in the car it was not the same. The misty solitude of yesterday was now forever in the past.

Halfway down the high street of a small forgettable market town with the wonderfully memorable Viking name of Thirsk, Neil suddenly told me to stop, and I pulled sharply into the kerb. He jumped out of the car without a word, slamming the door behind him, and ran back down the street to a hardware shop. I thought for a moment about following him but decided that I spent too much time shambling along after him. So instead I stayed in the car and pulled out a crumpled Marlboro from the box I had hurriedly stuffed into my pocket so that my mother wouldn't find it while I was gone. (Dad had recently died of lung cancer and I was trying to hide from her the shameful fact that I was a smoker, even though my habit was ridiculously light compared to his regular forty-year twenty-a-day consumption.) The tar tasted good, and I let the smoke roll around the corners of my mouth before sucking it into my lungs then out again in a slim smooth gust onto the Figaro's windscreen, where it billowed and dispersed. A few more mouthfuls and I had to crack the window open to stop my eyes from watering. All the time, I looked nervously up the street and back in my mirrors for a traffic warden, but there was none. I tapped absently on the dashboard for a while, until suddenly the door opened and Neil crashed in with a big smile, a large plastic bag bulging with cans of some kind, and a blast of cold Yorkshire air.

'Let's go!' he said, so urgently that I thought for a moment he had robbed the shop. But nobody followed us as I pulled out and sped up the high street, and Neil's face was excited rather than nervous. As we left Thirsk behind, he pulled a large screwdriver out of the bag and began urgently prying open the lid of what I now saw was a can of bright pink paint.

'Look, if you want to do a paint job on the Figaro, you have to do it properly,' I said. 'That stuff's not designed for cars. It'll just wash right off.'

Neil laughed. 'A paint job's a good idea,' he said, 'but that's not what I had in mind. Just keep driving. All will soon become clear.' He kept fiddling with the can, until he had the lid fully off and the pink paint was slopping around exposed to the air. I tried to keep my eyes on the road and to trust Neil but it was difficult.

'Stop!' he said suddenly, and I instinctively

thumped on the brake pedal, sending a miniature tidal wave of bright pink paint flooding over the edge of the can onto the floor of the Figaro.

Neil jumped out of the car, oblivious to the mess, and started running up the road with the can in his hand. Suddenly I saw what it was he had in mind. On the top of the hill stood a big yellow box, and beyond that the familiar series of little white lines on the road. Still running, Neil took a quick look over his shoulder, then scanned the horizon in all directions. Seeing nobody, he tipped the can up so that the thick florid paint sloshed joyously over the road, covering those tyrannical little white lines in a solid coating of Barbie pink. He did the same on the other side of the road before waving me forward.

'Yes, that's it, Jack, bring her in,' he said, hopping up and down with relentless excitement and energy. 'Now, be careful, now, yes, that's it, don't drive over the paint, they'll match your tyre patterns in a national database or some such malevolent dictatorial scheme. Yes. Slow now, don't speed, haw haw.'

His face was flushed and his dark eyes shone wildly; his hands were shaking so badly that he had to fumble with the door handle for several seconds. As soon as he was in I stamped on the accelerator and we sped off into the bright spring morning, the gaudy swatches of pink fading quickly in the rear-view mirror.

'That's what I'm talking about!' he shouted. 'Action and thought coming together in one beautiful moment. You could spend a whole life thinking about the oppressive, intrusive, unjust tyranny of having government cameras on every corner watching you and punishing you automatically for expressing one moment of individuality and freedom. And you could get more and more angry, and you could start vandalising phone boxes or smashing shop windows, as I did myself when I was of a certain young age and didn't know any better, but that's a longer and more tortuous story for another day entirely, or perhaps another lifetime. I never attacked old ladies, or stabbed other young angry people just like myself, but I can understand those acts as if I had done them myself. Action divorced from thought, Jack. You're angry at your parents or your school or your boss or society or the government, and you act your anger out on some poor bastard who just happens to be walking past, when what you really should be doing is shouting at your parents or your boss or starting a revolution to change all the things you disagree with.'

'Praxis,' I said.

'Quite. The people who run this whole show know that if people started to get their shit together and began acting meaningfully instead of in random disconnection from their real thoughts, feelings and knowledge, they wouldn't be able to throw us in jail or send us off to die or make us work overtime all our lives for the maintenance of a system that views us as driftwood. It's the same with all the people who hate their jobs and feel secretly trapped by their families, who try to solve their problems by buying a new pair of shoes. Action divorced from thought. The result's obvious: nobody's happy, except of course the company selling shoes.'

'Well, that's what matters, isn't it? That companies should be happy, even if people are not.'

Neil smiled. 'You got it, mate. Insane, isn't it?'

'It is,' I said. 'Well, anyway, I see another opportunity for praxis coming up just past that junction.'

'Yes!' Neil yelled. 'Let's go! Let's try it without stopping. You just cruise through the centre of the road, and I'll lean out here making the best possible use of the Figaro's open-top design to pour my paint out in a beautiful pink dollop over their fascist little white lines.'

It worked, reasonably well. He started a bit too soon on the first set of lines, but his aim and timing gradually improved. Our main problem was other drivers. As much as people complain about the draconian speed cameras, we couldn't be sure that they would view our project in the spirit of emancipation in which it was intended. So we had to either pull over and wait for a clear road in both directions, not a frequent sight in England these days, or just drive by and save our paint for the next one. The first option delayed us too much and made Neil, in particular, far too impatient. It was as if he needed the incessant motion of the car on the tarmac to fuel the stream of thoughts and chatter that made him happy. When the car ground to a halt, he too became sluggish and listless, looking around at all the vehicles streaming past and saying before long, 'Aw, come on Jack, let's just get going again and get 'em next time.' And as soon as we felt again the roar of the engine and the rumble of the tyres on the road, the fresh cold wind rushing over our heads, he would be happy once more and would watch the green hills, farms and villages speeding past us and launch another long soliloquy about some book that had changed his life.

Soon we were back on the A1 again. Up here the dark drear of the Holloway Road was far away. It was a big, wide, open, straight old Roman road. It had been called Dere Street, as I discovered later on, although I'm not sure where that came from because surely in Latin it would have been Via Derus or some such thing, so why give an English name as the Roman name for a Roman road? Anyway, it is now called Leeming Lane, or to most bored commuters and travelling salesmen just the plain old A1. It took us north with a speed and uncomplicated, unfussy directness that initially delighted Neil. 'This is it!' he shouted out into the wind. 'Now we're really moving!' But there was also a steady stream of cars, lorries and coaches doing exactly sixty-miles-an-hour, and being in this stream felt not like driving but like being on a very fast conveyor belt.

It also made our project of unrestrained vandalism almost impossible. We passed three or four speed cameras without taking any action, but the traffic showed no sign of thinning so at the fifth one we decided to pull over and just wait as long as it took. The cars sped past us in both directions for an interminable length of time, rocking our little Figaro each time with the force of the air they had displaced. Neil grew more and more agitated, and I suggested just moving on and waiting until we got to a quieter road.

'Here, look,' I said, showing him the big tattered old atlas on which I'd planned our trip for long nights at home in Crouch End. Even years before I met Neil I had sat up late at night tracing the red and green lines all over Britain, planning the best route from London to Aberdeen or from Plymouth to Newcastle via Abergavenny; even though I suspect that without Neil my great British road trip would always have remained purely hypothetical. Anyway, I showed him the tattered old sheets of paper with the faded lines, and tried to explain how we could cut across onto the A66 and the A67, then skirt around Newcastle on the A68. But he wasn't interested. He tried to look at the map but his eyes were faded grey and his forehead was creased and crinkled.

'Fuck it!' he said finally, and gathered up the cans of paint and hurled them all out of the window into the hedgerow beside us.

'What are you doing?' I asked. 'We could have gone on to another one, on a quieter road, and — '

'What the fuck is the point? We can wait all day for a chance to paint over one set of little white lines on the road, and there'll still be a thousand more up and down the country that

72

we'll never get to. And even the ones we do manage to get to, they'll be out tomorrow morning with their teams of workmen and they'll scrape up our pink and paint right over it with their little white lines, and everything will be just as it was before.'

'But we'll have made a point.'

'To who? A few dozen motorists who won't really understand and will just view it as a funny little story to tell the wife when they get home? Fuck it.'

We sat there arguing for a few minutes as the cars swished loudly past and our little Figaro rocked from side to side with the speed and violence of it all. I said he was shallow and gave up too easily, and he said I was naïve if I believed that two people as tiny as us could change a single thing against the crushing weight of 60 million people's utter inertia. We were busy tearing into each other, and I was on the point of getting out of the car to retrieve the paint myself, when suddenly we noticed the blue lights that had been flashing behind us for some time, and I turned to stare at the burly black crotch of a policeman.

'We had an anonymous report of someone tipping rubbish out of a car along here,' the man said, bending down to shove his red stubbly face into my open window.

'Yes, yes, I think they went that way,' Neil said, leaning over in front of me and putting on his best smile.

'In a blue-green Figaro?' the policeman asked, a sarcastic smile spreading across his face.

'Yes, yes, that was it!' Neil said.

'Registration NL51 TPR?'

Neil was silent after that; he sat back in his seat and looked straight ahead, and I did the same. The policeman, too, was silent for a good few seconds, like a minor daytime soap-opera actor milking his handful of lines for everything they were worth. Then he proceeded with the formalities of a ticket and a £100 on-the-spot fine, and watched as we collected our bag from the hedge. He even walked around the car checking the tax disc, the state of the tyres and the lights, just to see if there was anything else he could get us for, probably in punishment for Neil's attempts to deceive him. But his efforts were thwarted — I had checked the car thoroughly (Neil said obsessively) before the trip, a habit I picked up from my father — so he just told us to behave ourselves from now on, and waddled back to his car, using his flashing lights to get back into the stream of traffic while we sat there for a good few minutes more, impotently waiting for a gap.

5

Back in the stream of evenly-spaced sixty-mile-an-hour traffic on the long straight wide road, we sat silent. Neil's feet were crowded by the big bag of paint pots and, by then, even I had no desire to have them in the car anymore. Our paint-spraying spree had been naïve and futile, like throwing stones at a tank; but now, without it, our trip felt empty and worthless. Everything seemed dead for us. All that remained was the interminable sixty-mile-an-hour trundle north with a thousand other drones to a destination we no longer had any interest in reaching. The spring sun still shone as before, but the landscape looked flat and colourless. I lit a cigarette, and Neil asked for one too, and we both sat there inhaling tar and staring straight ahead at the back of a horsebox. The horse was hidden except for a small portion of its smooth brown flanks and a long black-haired tail hanging down outside the back of the trailer.

'Poor bastard,' said Neil. 'He can move two inches to the left, or two inches to the right, but any more than that and he comes up against cold hard metal.'

'Yeah,' I said, taking a long, sad drag on the cigarette and making myself cough.

'Even when he gets out of that box they'll put blinkers on him and keep him on a tight rein, so that all he can do is stare straight ahead and put one hoof in front of the other.'

'Yeah.'

'And even then he can only go as fast as he's told. If he drags his feet he gets a cane on his arse; then he gets over-excited and goes too fast and some cunt he can't see yanks at the bit between his teeth to pull him back.'

'Yeah.'

Silence blanketed us as we finished our cigarettes, staring blankly at the horse's tail slightly swishing. Then I saw a lay-by and pulled over next to an overflowing rubbish bin. Neil dumped the bag of paint on top but it tumbled off the precarious pile almost immediately, hitting the floor. The top came off one of the pots and bright pink paint spread all over the dark dank mud, giving new life to long-abandoned crisp packets and Coke cans. We were too tired to raise a smile.

From the lay-by it took five long minutes to find a gap in the traffic. A BMW with tinted windows roared its engine impatiently behind us, the driver honking his horn at every tiny gap, not understanding that a Figaro's little one-litre engine takes a lot longer to get up to sixty-miles-an-hour than his monstrous machine. Neil started muttering under his breath and I think he was about to get out of the car and start a fight when I finally lurched forward into a gap big enough to avoid a crash but not big enough to avoid angry honking from the driver behind me. Neil stuck a big upright finger through the open roof.

Everything seemed broken, and I only kept on driving north because I couldn't think of what else to do. The thought of the Holloway Road oppressed me even more than this long straight desolate road to nowhere, and so I kept trundling along at sixty-miles-an-hour, past empty fields and sleeping villages shielded behind high walls. The sun was low and orange.

As we passed a huge ugly cement factory, Neil reached back behind him and rummaged in his bag again. Soon the cassette was whirring once more and Matt Dillon twanged out the story of a real road trip, and the sound of the parties, girls and soulful wanderings through the vast open American landscape made our sad shuffle through the confines of little England seem pathetic.

'We should find a hotel,' I said.

'Fuck that,' Neil said. 'I want to be in

Scotland by sundown.'

I opened my mouth to argue, but knew it would be useless. I stared ahead at the back of a lorry. It had rained here earlier in the day and spray flew up. Suddenly I felt unbearably cold even with my coat on and a woolly hat over my head, so I pulled over to put the top back up before beginning the long slog up to Scotland.

We hit the edge of Newcastle's urban sprawl at rush-hour, and crawled along with a million other people as the sun went down. By now Sal Paradise was picking cotton in San Joaquin Valley with Terry. Neil was quiet this time, so I could let the words wash over my tired brain, and soon my mind was not on the murky outskirts of Newcastle in the cold March dusk, but in the sunshine and possibilities of southern California. I remembered reading the book, a silver Penguin Classics paperback edition, when I was a teenager, and falling in love with the world of hitching and kicks, cabooses and pickups, Oklahoma farmers and San Francisco hipsters, a world so far from my own. This was a world without rules or expectations, a world that seemed to roll along with the wheels of a black '47 Cadillac or a mud-spattered Hudson, its boundaries constantly shifting, its parameters changing with each new town clocked up on the long trek back and forth across the huge open continent. It was a world of memorable characters encountered by chance, like Mississippi Gene the freight-train-riding hobo, and Eddie the Irish track driver, and Okie Frankie, and Montana Slim. And of course Dean Moriarty himself, who I wanted to be for a couple of years from about thirteen to fifteen, even though in my heart I knew I was not and never could be so free and spontaneous, and it was in trying and failing to be Dean Moriarty that I discovered for the first time in my life the limits of being human — that wanting to be something did not make it so.

Then I grew up and got used to my limitations, and I learned in school to scorn Kerouac as a writer who could only tell one story in one style, a circular tale of hope and hopelessness that bore no comparison to more subtle, complex, challenging, heavily-footnoted works translated from the original Kikuyu, which could only be understood by clever people who had read every book worth reading and could thus understood the context of every line of obscure prose — and explain it to their students in long heavily-footnoted books full of jargon that you needed to have read lots of other long heavily-footnoted books to decipher. And as these tedious, inelegant books began to make sense to me, I felt educated and validated, and began to produce tedious, inelegant, erudite prose of my own. However, as my cub-scout leader told me one dark November evening when we were out in the woods, when humans become lost their instinct is to go in circles. Historically having been pack animals, their intuition tells them that circles will return them to the safety of the fold rather than send them off on a long isolated trip into the unknown. Despite my education, I found myself circling regularly back to this simple, circular tale, searching for what Sal and Dean were searching for and, like them, never quite finding it or even knowing what it was.

When we stopped for petrol, Neil offered to drive the rest of the way. I hesitated and started muttering about insurance considerations, but he assured me that he had insurance that covered him to drive anybody's car. Although I didn't believe his promises for a second, I felt they somehow released me from my obligation to worry and so I agreed, relieved to take a break after a day's long and somewhat harrowing driving.

'Alright, here we go; you'll see what driving is all about now,' Neil said, and he hopped into the driver's seat while I went off to pay and buy some packaged food from the brightly-lit, freezing-cold Tesco Express. He was already revving the engine when I walked back across the dark slick forecourt, and I had barely shut the door before the Figaro lurched forward and swung around to the left, clattered over a speed bump, rolled smoothly over to the right, hugging the kerb tightly, and accelerated out into the straight lane back to the main road. The freshly-fuelled engine gave everything it could to Neil and roared up to sixty by the time it reached the end of the slip-road. With a quick flash of his indicators and a hand stuck out of the window, Neil slipped straight back into the stream of traffic, flipping his outstretched hand into a quick thumbs-up before pulling it back in to grip the steering wheel with two fingers while his left hand rested restlessly on the gear stick, itching to change up even though it was only a three-speed automatic gearbox and was already in top gear.

All the way up the A1, as orange faded to black, my eyelids were peeled back in fear. Neil drove with a restless energy, always revving the engine and nosing the bumper up close to that of the car in front, constantly nudging out over the centre line and leaning over to peer ahead into the glaring headlights of the oncoming traffic, searching for a break that would allow him to nip out and around the car in front. Here we were, constantly looking to slip ahead one place in the long sixty-mile-an-hour queue of cars that snaked back all the way from Scotland down to the choking traffic lights of London, where by the time it hit Archway and the Holloway Road it would have slowed to the familiar snarling snorting rush-hour crawl. Only once or twice in the first hour did he find such a gap, and when he did he slammed the gearstick joyously down into second, and the Figaro roared, whined and jumped into the opposite lane, straining to inch past the car in front before the bright white headlights of the next oncoming vehicle got too close. I looked across once at the driver of the Mercedes we were overtaking, a youngish woman who was just staring in disbelief at this comical old Figaro straining to pass her; she caught my eye for a second and in that second I think she somehow understood that Neil was mad and that the safest thing to do was simply to ease off the accelerator and let him slip in ahead of her. Not for a second on that long trip north could I take my eyes off the road, and neither did Neil. In fact, although he sat quite far back in his seat and held the wheel casually with only two fingers of one hand, it was clear that his every muscle was tensed, every cell and sinew in his body working to pour his entire energy and being into the wheel, the pedals, the gearstick and the road.

As we passed Alnwick and pressed on into the old Marches, the cars thinned out and Neil was able to overtake more easily and to pour forward at greater speed. Nevertheless, despite all the sound and fury of his driving, our progress didn't seem to be much faster than it would have been had we just trundled along at sixty with everyone else. The stretches of camera-less traffic-less road were short, and any time spent barrelling along at seventy or eighty was usually negated by a spell stuck behind a bus or truck going at fifty. We covered the seventy miles from Newcastle to the Scottish border in a little more than an hour. I didn't mention this to Neil, however. As scared as I was of his driving, I was happy that he had found a purpose again. I couldn't bear it when he became listless. I wanted him to believe that he was getting us somewhere fast, even if neither of us was sure of exactly where we were going.

At around eight o'clock we crossed the border, a moment that would easily have been missed if we weren't both paying such avid attention to the road. There were none of the usual accoutrements of borders — no barriers, huts, guards or fences. Just a small sign by the side of the road, as if we were crossing from Surrey to Sussex. No matter that Hadrian had built his wall or that the Picts had fought jealously to protect their independence for centuries while their feeble southern neighbours were overrun by everyone from Rome to Saxony, from Normandy to Trondheim, until they didn't know who they were anymore and had to create an identity by force. The long-guarded independence of this ancient land had been erased by stealth through the accident of a shared king and the crude deception of an Act of Parliament forced upon a-bought-and-paid-for local elite, and now it was nothing. It made me wonder why Neil and I had expended so much energy to get there.

At the first town we came to, a sleepy border town whose name I've forgotten, Neil pulled off the main road and for the first time gave the poor Figaro a break from his relentless demands, just letting the engine purr softly as we rolled into the centre of town.

'This place needs waking up!' Neil said, and gave one long loud honk on the horn. I laughed even as I was cringing inwardly. It was still early but this seemed like an early to bed, early to rise kind of place, and I worried that a horde of angry villagers would come out of their houses ready to send us scuttling home in our Figaro to think again. In the end, though, there was no visible response. We kept on trundling down the deserted high street, until at the far end we saw a little cluster of lights, which, as we got closer, turned out to be a big old country pub, the kind of majestic wood-beamed place that had clearly once been a major staging-post on the road north, with stables and multiple sprawling bars, and accommodation for dozens of weary travellers. Now, however, it had been bypassed by the slick wide road sweeping around the edge of town and superseded by the bright lights of the Travelodge on the main road, and catered these days to a dwindling crowd of aging locals. In a few years all of these old places will be gone. In the cities they're converted to nightclubs or knocked down to make way for luxury apartment blocks, and in old irrelevant bypassed border towns they're left to rot and decay into dark skeletons overgrown with weeds. For now, though, this one was limping along, and we entered its tired old carpeted interior. There was even the musty brown head of some long-dead stuffed animal hung on the wall as a trophy.

'That policeman's probably hung your

head on his wall by now,' Neil said with a hearty but hollow laugh, jutting his neck out and staring in glassy-eyed imitation of the moose or elk, or whatever poor creature it was.

'Which one?' I asked glumly. 'I've been stopped twice and caught speeding once. That's more involvement with the law in two days than I've had in my entire life.'

Neil smiled and cheerfully led me into the bar. He bought me a pint of frothy warm ale in an old-fashioned pewter tankard and a big plate of greasy chips, and we clunked tankards and drank quickly to erase the memory of our long hard day. One great quality, I thought then, that Neil had was the big-hearted acceptance of other people's experiences as utterly valid and not worth putting down in any way. He could well have scoffed at my feeble anxiety over a couple of minor traffic offences and started relating a whole long story about his string of court cases and ASBOs and stints in reform school. But he understood in some important way that although everyone is essentially the same, we are also as different as can be, and can never truly understand someone else or his life experiences. Forgetting our early argument in the car, I thought that he accepted such differences as natural and, although he would spend hours relentlessly trying to convince me of the deep truth of some half-thought-out theory he had concocted from his sporadic reading of philosophical and literary texts, he never tried to force his experience on me or belittle me for who I was. I warmed to him every time I noticed this, and so we passed a very happy hour or two in that pub at a small wooden corner table, with the fire crackling behind us and the handful of locals eyeing us suspiciously from behind their dark tankards.

'Let's get going again!' Neil said suddenly, just as I was ready to settle in for the night.

'Go where?' I asked fuzzily.

'North. As far north as we can go before the land runs out altogether and wild grey tossing seas stretch out ever further north to dim distant islands populated only by the hard, rough-skinned descendants of Vikings. Come on, we're in Scotland already. What's the point of just staying in some border town drinking weak beer out of pewter tankards and getting stared at? We must keep going, Jack, we really must.'

I pointed out all kinds of practical considerations like the time, now almost ten o'clock, the darkness, the poor roads further north, the unpredictable weather, the not entirely reliable engine of my Figaro, the warmth and comfort of the bar, the reasonable prices of the Travelodge on the main road, and most importantly and urgently of all, the fact that we were well into our third pint of beer and even if we could drive safely, which was doubtful, drinking and driving was the kind of thing that could get us not just ticketed but thrown in jail. All of this practicality, however, he waved away casually like a horse flicking its tail to rid itself of flies. He would drive, he said, and with the window down the cold Scottish night air would slap him awake and sober by the time we got back to the main road. I could crawl in the back, push our bags onto the floor and stretch out to sleep off my beer and fatigue, and by the time I woke up he would be all ready for a break himself and we could switch over, repeating the trick through the night as often as necessary until we made it to the place where the Northern Lights flash like Roman candles and the cold hard sea lashes the shore.

He continued in this vein as we finished off our beer, using ever more florid and extravagant language, until I almost started to believe that a soggy, windswept stretch of dark anonymous seashore was Nirvana, the land of milk and honey, the Holy Grail and the pot of gold at the end of our long dark lonely quest.

Of course it was no such thing. There is only one true ending in life; all the others are much-anticipated anticlimaxes.

We slogged through the cold dark night along ever narrower roads, Neil gunning the engine and working the steering so aggressively that I slept only fitfully in the back seat, a long confused fit of dozing interrupted by the white flash of headlights, the lurch of the car to left or right that sent my head or feet crashing into the door, or the occasional beep of a horn and the constant churning and whining of my poor old Figaro's tired little one-litre engine. At some point up around Perth, I woke up groggy and confused and staggered out into overwhelming blackness to be whipped by the wind for a few seconds before diving in to take over the wheel. Neil retreated to the back seat, snoring loudly as soon as his head hit the padded leather seat. If there is a God, He is the only one who knows how I stayed awake that night and didn't hit anything or anybody. The window was open and the harsh north wind stung my face, and the road was lonely and deserted from Perth up through the Highlands to where it met the sea again near Inverness. But still my soul felt empty and hollow and my parched throat ached for coffee, none of which we would find up that long dark road north. Fortunately Neil had filled up with petrol near Edinburgh because, for mile after mile on that road, the only service stations I passed were shuttered and dark.

Hunger tore at me. The plastic food from the Tesco Express was long gone, and the greasy pub chips had done little more than soak up the beer. As I stared ahead at the two white cones of light flashing onto the dark road for mile after mile after lonely mile, the aching hunger and the bitter cold rushing in through the open window made me feel like a weary traveller of yesteryear, braving the worst of the night and the ravages of cold, hunger and fatigue to get where I wanted to go. I understood something of Neil's crazed rationale. A comfortable night in a Travelodge and a leisurely cruise up the coast in the bright light of morning with the windows up and the heater on would not seem like travelling.

This cold dark windswept slog reminded me of mystical narratives full of coaches and horses with steaming breath, and cartwheels splashing through mud and changing horses at a roadside inn before plunging ever onwards through the night, feeling every inch, foot, yard and furlong of the journey because there was no choice but to feel it. Now that we can tune it all out with radios, heaters, air conditioning, fast cars and smooth roads we feel the lack of something we can't put our fingers on. Well, as I journeyed through the night, battered by the wind, my hands gripping the wheel through every twist, every turn, every pothole and puddle, hearing the roar of the engine and the grinding of wheels on tarmac and the occasional distant sound of animals in the vast night, I understood why Neil had felt the perverse impulse to spurn comfort and practicality in favour of a taste of old-fashioned hardship.

The road hugged the craggy coast for the last section, up through tiny ancient settlements like Brora, Helmsdale and Wick. Neil was driving now; I had given up on trying to sleep and was propped up in the passenger seat trying to stare out into the big black void and think big thoughts, but always finding my eyes drawn back to the narrow tunnel of light that spewed out from the front of the car. The road was hilly and the Figaro was starting to sputter and complain, but it kept chugging valiantly along through all the steep rises and plunging valleys.

I put the next cassette in the deck and Matt Dillon's voice filled the night with tales of crossing the great Mississippi River on the Algiers ferry. For the first time, our journey felt like more than just a pale shadow of the great quest of Sal and Dean. Perhaps it was because we were beyond the grey confines of England and up in the wild open heights of Scotland, or perhaps it was simply that it was dark and the drab cement factories and sad brick towns were hidden by the night. Whatever the reason, our journeys felt comparable suddenly, and as I listened to Matt Dillon twanging out the tale of Dean and Sal causing havoc with Old Bull Lee in Louisiana I felt a stronger connection than at any time since my teenage years curled up in my bedroom reading and rereading the slim silver volume until I fell asleep with it on my chest and picked it up again for a couple of deliciously fantastic hours before the drudgery of breakfast and school.

I felt close not only to Sal and Dean and Old Bull Lee but also to my former self, that shy tortured teenager suffocating under a weight of expectations. The world had seemed limitless and terrifying in those days. I was top of my class in every subject, and my class was in the top stream at one of the best public schools in London. It was presumed by teachers, parents, uncles and aunts that I would be a success, a prognosis that I never thought to question. All that remained was to choose which field I would excel in. Law or finance, academia or politics? I had shrugged off all these questions with a teenage grunt that meant 'Haven't decided yet' while my soul secretly yearned to be a traveller, a teller of tales, a free spirit roaming from town to town and country to country. I'd vaguely planned to set off around Europe following the harvest, making enough money picking grapes in the Dordogne to pay my way to southern Italy for the olive harvest, then to Athens to teach English through the winter, and so on in meticulously planned routes across huge continents and through enticing cities until I ran out of places to go.

But the trip was postponed for exams, holiday jobs, internships, university and a thousand other distractions, and soon it was too late to attempt it — so full of common sense had I been filled. Now on this cold dark night rushing pointlessly through Scotland I had once again found the courage to abandon sense, or perhaps more accurately I had lacked the courage to resist Neil's imposition of senselessness upon me, and the result was a few hours of pure happiness of being.

Neil was quiet and tense all the time, one hand on the wheel and the other on the automatic gearstick, looking ahead at the road and beyond it to the North Star, and only muttering occasionally about the North-ern Lights, which he desperately wanted to see but was not blessed with on this particular night.

We swapped places again near Wick, not realising in our hazy semi-consciousness that it was only a short tortuous drive from there to the little cluster of houses that signalled John O'Groats. We found our way through the streets to park in a little spot right by the sea. In the absolute darkness, the water was impossible to distinguish from the sky or the land, but we knew it was out there in the vastness. We could smell the salt in the air and, when I brought the Figaro to a halt on the side of the road and switched off the engine, we could hear the angry crash of waves. After so many hours with the rumble of the Figaro in my ears, the waves sounded strangely sharp and for a few seconds before my brain adjusted I could hear the accompanying silence as a distinct sound.

Neil looked at me smiling, then jumped out of the car and yelled, 'Race you to the sea!' And he was off into the night. All I could do was jump out, absurdly pausing to lock the car as if there was anyone else crazy enough to be awake within a hundred miles of us on that dark freezing night in the far, far north, and follow him.

I could not pick out his silhouette but could hear his big feet pounding the shingly beach somewhere up ahead, and followed in a mad, blind run. I trusted that the beach would not throw up any rocks in my path because, in that absolute darkness, I would not have seen anything — even right beneath my feet. Fortunately it was a smooth downward slope until, just as I could sense the sea only a yard or two ahead of me, I tripped over the big soft bulk of Neil, sitting on the pebbles untying his shoelaces. I went face-first over the top of him, and he laughed and grabbed me by the waist to hold me up. Finally, I slumped down beside him and asked if he was completely out of his mind.

'Yes, yes!' he shouted at the waves. 'I'm out of my mind with the overwhelming and irresistible urge to cast myself out into that dark ancient sea. Of course I can't go in right up to the neck as I really want to because, as I am sure you will tell me, I could catch pneumonia on a night like this. But I am going to roll up my trousers and paddle and splash about like I used to when I was eight-years-old, and you're going to join me, Jack, because you have no choice and you know as well as I do that if you resist I will drag you into that icy salt water, clothes and all, and your shoes and socks will be soaking wet for the rest of the night and day and probably the following night too.'

I knew it, and didn't doubt he would do it. Soon my shoes were off, my socks were balled up inside them and my trousers were rolled up to the knee. Neil waited for me and then grabbed my hand firmly and led me to the sea. Together we stepped forward where the beach sloped away and felt the first wave of icy water crash onto our feet; we yelped and screamed and laughed but gripped each other tight by the hand so that neither of us could step back. Another step forward and we sank down to our shins, and another and another, and the water was up around our knees, soaking the rolled-up bottoms of our trousers, numbing us below the knees and for a moment I worried that we would buckle and tumble senseless into the sea. The waves were strong but not too violent, and after we accustomed ourselves to the iciness of the water we stood quite comfortably. Soon the rhythmical slush slosh slush of the waves became quite peaceful.

'Are you awake now?' Neil yelled.

'Wooooo!' I replied.

'Nothing up ahead until you get to the North Pole,' Neil shouted. 'Look at the stars spread out before us, watching us two lonely souls down here and probably thinking how crazy we are!'

I looked up and saw what he meant,

although the night was partially cloudy and the array was not as brilliant as it would have been on some other nights. Still, I could see why the ancients thought the stars were gods and gave them names. It did feel as if a great interstellar audience was spread out before us in a vast cosmic amphitheatre and as a result I suddenly felt very small and very, very cold.

'Let's go back,' I said, tugging at Neil's hand. To my surprise he did not resist, and we turned round, picked up our shoes and went on back up the beach, which seemed steeper than it had as we'd careened down it, still holding hands all the way back to the car.

Somewhere I had packed a towel, but there was no time to look for it. Our feet were so numb that we began to totter and sway like drunkards as we neared the car. We desperately switched on the engine, flicked the heaters up to maximum, waited for a couple of long, long minutes for the heat to kick in and then held our feet up in front of the delicious rush of hot air until we could feel our blood begin to flow again.

Neil laughed and joked all the while but I could see the same fear in his eyes as I felt myself — the awful sense for a minute or two that we had gone too far, had pushed ourselves beyond our limitations and would suffer pain, frostbite, even amputation as a punishment for an arrogance that our interstellar audience had surely not witnessed since the days of Canute.

6

I woke up suffocating. We had left the engine running and the heaters on and both fallen asleep looking out at what had been blackness and stars, but was now the North Sea. I shut off the engine, opened the door and let icy air blast through the fug, jolting Neil awake. He responded with a, 'Hum, huh? Shut that door, shut that door!' Wiping some dribble from his stubbly chin, he looked ahead and said, 'Ah, a beautiful sight, that.'

I looked out at the blue-orange cloud-studded sky and saw some beauty there, but the sea was grey and angry. The beach on which we had run was a treacherous slippery slope of slick black rocks sliding down into a mass of frothy grey water lashing petulantly at the shore. To the left and right the land rose into small ragged cliffs. On one cliff the silhouette of a man or woman stood bundled against the cold, holding a leash and facing out to sea. Otherwise all was deserted and felt as if it had been for many hundreds of years, even though we knew that in a couple of hours hordes of blistered backpacked hikers would arrive to take photographs of themselves as proof that they had completed a walk across Britain for the benefit of some charity to which people would have given money anyway if left to their own devices. An hour or two later the tea-drinking day-trippers would follow, taking their own photographs to be added to albums that would sit in an attic among broken clocks and dusty unfashionable paintings waiting for the day when their children or grandchildren hired a junk-shop dealer to sort through them for anything worth selling.

'I'm glad we got here at night,' I said.

Neil smiled. 'I'm always right, Jack. You always grumble and complain and tell me I'm mad, and then follow along anyway and have the time of your life. You should just skip the grumbling and complaining part and go straight to the enjoyment.'

'I'll try,' I said, but we both knew I was lying. If I spent a lifetime with Neil I would never be like him any more than he would be like me. The thought saddened me beyond belief as I stared out at the big grey sea.

'Let's go,' I said.

The trouble with getting across the length of Britain in two days is that there's nowhere further to go. Neil was all for finding a ferry up to the Orkneys or Shetlands, or some such strange windswept adventure, but after a night of cold air rushing through the window, topped off with a dip in an icy March sea, I was feeling a deep chill in my chest and craved the warmth of towns, buses, pubs and streetlights. So for an hour or two we toured aimlessly around barren, hilly, narrow country roads while the sun rose higher in the sky and clouds closed in around it, until a grimy little white-walled café appeared out of the morning gloom and we found something we could agree on.

Inside it was smoky, steamy and greasy, and packed with large, muscular men sitting wide-legged at tables that seemed too small for them. Some read newspapers; others attacked huge plates of fried bacon, sausages, fried bread and chips.

Nobody spoke, though a few eyes glanced over the tops of their newspapers as we walked in. The latest Beyoncé single jangled along with the sizzling of lard. There was no decoration except a string of forlorn gold tinsel across one wall that nobody had bothered to take down. The menu, handwritten on a piece of paper taped to the wall, consisted of three items: Set 1, Set 2 or Set 3. We both chose Set 3, on the basis that it cost 50p more and so would presumably provide a slightly bigger pile of greasy food than the other two.

'Tea or coffee?' the young waitress asked, looking bored.

'Tea,' I said.

'Coffee,' Neil said.

'White bread or brown?'

'White,' Neil said.

'Brown,' I said.

The waitress looked up from her pad. 'Don't think we've got any brown.'

'White, then,' I said.

A few minutes later she reappeared bearing heavy china plates loaded with glistening hunks of meat, eggs, bread, mushrooms, tomatoes, beans and chips.

'You must have strong forearms,' I said.

'What?' she asked, her blank pale-blue eyes looking limply back at me. 'Oh yeah. Thanks. You want any ketchup?'

I shook my head, but Neil nodded. When she returned, he put on a sweet smile and said, 'Thank you, my dear, thank you. Now what my friend here meant to say is that you have the most beautiful eyes he has seen in this long trip we've taken across the whole length of Britain. He's a little tired so it didn't come out right, but that's what he meant. Beautiful, limpid pools of — '

'Do you want anything else, then?' she asked, and scurried off.

Neil sighed. 'You know, I wanted to take

that girl and invite her along with us to drive all down to Cornwall or up to the Shetlands or across to Glasgow or wherever it is we're going. But she is scared of me, and for what? So now she will stay here in this greasy little room serving sausage and chips to a bunch of apes who would rather read the football scores than pay any attention to her.'

A few eyes flicked up at the word 'apes', but I buried my gaze in my plate of food and prayed that no trouble would start and indeed it didn't. When we were halfway through our breakfasts, Neil overheard someone talking about a rig and looked up suddenly.

'An oil rig? You all work on an oil rig?'

'We do. That's why we're not the friendliest bunch this morning. Just had our time on shore and now it's back to sea.'

'Well that's amazing, I mean truly amazing. I have always absolutely dreamed of working on an oil rig out in the big grey lonely sea, with just hard work to do in the bitter wind. Nothing to distract me or make me soft and weak like I get when I'm around city boys — no offence, Jack, my old friend. I think that fate has conspired or inspired us to be here at this exact moment; my friend Jack and I all beaten down and worn out from travelling around the roads of Britain for no great purpose, and you here ready to go off for long months at sea, which is exactly what we need in order to cleanse our bodies and minds from all the layers of dust and decay.'

The rig worker looked at Neil and then at me, then back to his plate smeared with the glistening remains of egg, bacon gristle and tomato sauce. 'I could get you a form for the next time,' he said slowly, still looking at his plate.

'Aw, no, next time is too late, we absolutely must leave with you this very morning. We're hard workers, strong as you can see — my friend Jack here is a member of a very exclusive health and fitness club in north London and has been known to expend huge amounts of energy there from time to time; while I have grown up in the unfortunate position of having to use my muscles on a daily basis to defend and establish myself in the cruel world of a south London housing estate and from there various institutions of hate, pure hate, my friend. So I am quite confident we could handle anything you throw at us.'

'I'm not saying you can't,' the man said. 'It just doesn't work like that anymore. You have to apply, and be interviewed, and take a test. It helps if you have qualifications.'

Neil bristled. He rolled up his sleeve,

slapped a rough hand around his meaty forearm and said, 'There are my qualifications. You want to feel them?'

The man leaned back in his chair and forced his eyes up from his plate to meet Neil's. He was a huge spiky-haired, rough-shaven hulk of a man, a fact he had kept hidden slightly by his hunched posture and timid demeanour. Now that I saw him full on, I glanced around the room at a dozen other men paying surreptitious attention, and began to feel afraid.

'Listen, pal,' he said. 'I didn't make the rules. I'd hire you if it was up to me, but it's not, OK? You can come with us if you want and speak to the rig manager, but you'll be wasting your time.'

'We'll come,' Neil said. 'We'll come. I'll talk to this manager about what I can do. I'll prove I can do it. I'll tell him if I don't work hard enough for his liking, he can toss me into the sea and let me swim back.'

There were some laughs from the surrounding tables. The atmosphere softened. 'You need experience, that's all,' said a young pale man with thinning hair. 'I'm just a roustabout, the lowest of the low. I get sent out in a storm to fix a cable or carry a crate from one side of the rig to the other. And I had to do an apprenticeship for that.'

'Yeah, and don't forget the offshore survival and fire-fighting course,' said another. 'That's mandatory before they'll even let you on the rig. Health and Safety.'

'And it helps if you have an SVQ,' said the first man. 'Offshore Drilling Operations Level One, or something equivalent. That'll help you move up faster. You could make roughneck or maybe derrickman in a year or two.'

From all around now men started adding their cautions and warnings and advice, and all the while Neil sank into a deeper and deeper depression, sitting for a long time with a piece of dry egg dangling from his fork just an inch from his mouth, before letting it fall onto the plate. Eventually, he put his fork down altogether and just listened to the men talking about what they'd had to go through to get their jobs and how hard it was to keep them and how long they had to survive just doing more and more training and not getting paid for it. He didn't seem to bear any malice towards the rig workers; in fact, he seemed a little sorry for them. Nevertheless, I was afraid of what he would do or say.

'What *could* we do for casual labour around here?' I asked quickly.

There was much murmuring and head-shaking. 'No, no, nothing around here,' said

106

one. 'Barely enough jobs for the locals. You're better off going back down south to the cities. More work there.'

Neil slammed his mug down, sending the murky contents slopping over the scratched plastic table. 'We *came* from the south,' he shouted. 'The south is what we're trying to get away from. Cameras on every corner, no room to move or to breathe, police just waiting for the next act of individuality so they can bag you and tag you and throw you away. A thousand jobs on every high street but all of them so emasculating that you're better off on the dole.'

He looked to me for support, but I said nothing. I just looked at him, marvelling at how he could be at once so menacing and so childlike, while pleading with my eyes for him to shut up.

'A job's a job,' one of the men muttered bitterly. 'Up here we don't have the luxury to pick and choose.'

'You think we do? You think it's a choice whether to work pouring lattes or scanning shampoo or scooping fried chicken into a paper bucket? It's the same shit, different colour. Always someone else getting rich off you, and the boss looking over your shoulder while you take a piss to make sure you don't take too long or drip on his floor.'

'It's hard work on the rig,' said the first man. 'Harder than anything you've ever done. But try supporting a family of five when you're out of work. Can't be done. We work and we're thankful for it.'

Amid the murmurs of assent, Neil looked at the ceiling in anger. 'Thankful?' he shouted finally, silencing them all. 'Thankful for the crumbs your boss tosses you as he makes millions from the oil you pump?' He looked at me again, and again I gave him nothing. 'We thought it'd be different up here,' he said a little sadly now. 'We just thought it'd be wilder, less controlled, more free.'

'Listen, pal, we're not a fucking zoo,' said the biggest man in the group, one who had been silent until now. 'You want an exotic species, keep going north until you see some penguins. Otherwise, fuck off down south where you belong.'

Neil jumped onto the table, kicking the plates to the floor where, instead of shattering as I'm sure he intended, they just bounced limply on the grease-soaked lino. Nevertheless, he looked like some primeval warrior or modern-day action figure as he stood there on the table with his legs crouched and his arms primed for a fight. His bloodshot eyes bulged alarmingly as he gazed around the room, daring anyone to come for him. He taunted the rig workers with some long string of nationalistic insults that I can't remember now and that, in any case, Neil never believed for a moment. He just wanted to fight, and the rig workers were the only people within reach.

I hardly recognised this version of him, the Neil of the harsh south London housing estate, the Neil that had got expelled from school and then collected ASBOs and cautions as I had collected football stickers. I had only ever got occasional glimpses of this Neil as he tried to pick fights in the cold darkness of the Holloway Road. This Neil scared me and fascinated me at once. He was, for me, the exotic creature, more colourful and deadly than anything I'd known before. I yearned for his infrequent appearances and then, when he appeared, instantly wanted him gone. He was too different, too unrecognisable.

It was the idea of this Neil that I liked, but as a reality I preferred the idealistic pub philosopher, the insatiable searcher for knowledge and freedom. When I saw Neil with muscles flexed, eyes bulging and veins pulsing in his shaven head, I got the lurching sense of being on a rollercoaster and just wanted to shut my eyes and wait for the end.

Fortunately, though, the men in the café

just gazed at him with a slightly bemused interest, as if he were a TV show. It didn't seem to occur to any of them to participate in this crazy performance.

'Let's go, Neil,' I whispered urgently into the silence. 'Nobody wants to fight you.'

'That fat fucker there sounded like he wanted to a minute ago,' Neil replied, his voice cracking a little as he pointed a shaky finger at the biggest man in the room.

'I told you to fuck off,' the man replied calmly. 'Very different thing. I've got a wife, three kids, a good job. I'm not going to lose them over you.'

'You're a slave!' Neil blurted. 'All of you. Scared to live because you might lose the little piece of shit your boss has let you grab hold of.'

There was silence. The show had lost their interest; they saw how it would end now, and they were just waiting for us to leave. Finally, I coaxed Neil down from the table and sent him outside while I paid up, leaving a generous tip for the insipid waitress.

From the café we followed the road south, back the way we had come on that long crazy night of thrashing through the darkness to reach the northern shore. We played the cassette a little more, but the stories of parties and hitching just depressed us, as all we seemed capable of doing was going right back the way we had come. When it came to the end of the tape, neither of us turned it over.

'He was right,' Neil said. 'We don't belong here.'

'Where then?' I replied. 'France? Thailand? Botswana?'

'Nowhere,' Neil said. 'We belong nowhere.'

'Maybe we belong in the past,' I offered. 'Maybe we're in the wrong time.'

'Past wasn't so great,' Neil muttered. 'Great for a few people, but the other 99 percent were pushing ploughs or digging coal.'

'The future, then,' I said weakly, and Neil just looked at me with a mixture of sympathy and irritation.

The miles clicked by, but with no sense of purpose now. After thirty or forty wasted miles, the silence became truly oppressive. I wondered if I should apologise for not backing Neil up with his ridiculous provocations in the café, but I got the sense that he'd forgotten that already, and I didn't want to remind him. I consoled myself with the thought that if things had turned violent, I would have stood beside him and fought the futile fight until the roustabouts and roughnecks had mauled every inch of my body. I don't know if I believed it even then, but being thoroughly beaten seemed a fitting outcome; more fitting than the real-life anti-climax, and the thought of it gave me inexplicable comfort.

Neil switched on the radio and bland pop songs circled around the car, interspersed with cheery comments from a DJ sounding exactly like the DJs in London but with a faint, watery Scottish accent. At least that gave us something to talk about for a few minutes. We chatted on about the way radio DJs sound the same whether you're in London, Bristol, the Scottish Highlands or Tennessee. We even laughed a little bit, as Neil did his best impression of a mellifluous baritone pouring feel-good banalities out onto the airwaves.

But soon we began to get the sense that we'd had that conversation before, and fell silent. Even the bright spring sun, the wild grey coastline and the occasional glimpses of the sea failed to brighten our mood. I felt an urge to turn off this road and go somewhere else, anywhere else, because following it meant ending up back on the dark, dirty Holloway Road with the other pale drunks. I wanted to follow a road all the way to the horizon and beyond it to mountains, deserts and wide, roaring blue oceans. I wanted to have adventures, surprises, and what Sal

Paradise quaintly called 'kicks'. But I couldn't think of anything that didn't make me feel tired and empty.

'Perhaps we left it too long,' I said. 'Perhaps you have to be younger to do this stuff. Like a dumb eighteen-year-old for whom anything beyond his Playstation is an amazing adventure, not jaded twenty-somethings who've seen everything already.'

I didn't believe it even as I was saying it, and Neil certainly didn't, but at least it kicked him out of his torpor for a while as he informed me that he had been travelling ever since he was spat out of Feltham Young Offenders Institution at sixteen, and even though he was now a few years older he felt no different.

'As a matter of fact,' he said, 'I have met some truly free spirits in all my wanderings and some of them have been two or three times my own age, but let me tell you, Jack, they had more freedom and life in their foreskins than those processed, packaged young university students have in their whole bodies as they choose their practical, useful subjects and courses to position themselves for lucrative and deadening careers making a hundred times as much money for their bosses as they do for themselves.'

Having been such a packaged entity at one

time myself and yet still having felt very much alive, I wanted to argue with Neil but couldn't find the energy. It was easier to let him go on, allowing the absolute certainty in everything he said to soothe my brow and make the world seem suddenly simpler than it had before he started speaking.

He moved on soon to a speech about one of these fifty-something 'free spirits' and I could tell he was back to life because he soon began interrupting himself with observations on the radio, the car, passing cars, people on the road, sheep, hills, odd-looking houses or the shape of the clouds, circling his way back unerringly from each digression, and sometimes from digressions within digressions, to find his way back to the original point. And he did it so seamlessly that it was hardly possible to tell the difference between his friend's mad beach party, the shape of a woman's breasts, the swoop of a gull and an off-the-cuff interpretation of the lyrics of R.E.M.'s *The Sidewinder Sleeps Tonite* that had just blasted cryptically out of the Figaro's crackly speakers. All seemed part of the same thing, integrally connected and quite natural to talk about in the same breath.

And that is not a cliché of the vulgar kind that Oscar might use in his romances: Neil did quite literally talk in the same breath for minutes at a stretch, not leaving even the slimmest of cracks between each word, so that a conversation with him seemed like just one long word running on for mile after mile and containing all the elements of a fully rounded story. This habit made it impossible to interrupt unless he wanted me to, or unless I actually talked over him, and even when I did that he would quite often just keep chattering on at the same time, letting his voice do battle with mine and with Michael Stipe's and whoever else happened to be around at the same time. He would almost always win, keeping on going and making his point until he had finished, when he'd say, 'Oh, hey, Jack, you wanted to say something back then, didn't you?' But by that time I had usually forgotten what I had tried to interject, or it had come to seem small and irrelevant, so I just shrugged, said it didn't matter and let him continue anew.

His voice comforted me more than the rumble of tyres on the road or the roar of the engine or the white line stretching out ahead of us, or the smooth segues of the DJ. When he was talking, I felt at peace and everything seemed to make sense — and even if it didn't I was quite happy with the world and my place in it. Only when his chattering dried up and I had to listen to the silence of my own soul did I begin to feel uneasy again, and I'd try to prod him cunningly into a new speech.

Near Aberdeen his enthusiasm began to dry up, and my hands went slack on the wheel. We realised that the night of madness had overtaken us and, as we were men, not gods, we would have to rest in the end. So we pulled into that dour town perched on the edge of the North Sea and searched in vain for something to divert us from our emptiness. The sandwich shops were of the lace-curtained, dry-bread and supermarket-ham variety, the handful of restaurants were closed, and the pubs looked more tired than we were. There was a cinema showing the latest American romantic comedy, but we knew we would fall asleep in that big empty darkness and wake up stiff and aching as some miserable teenager pointedly poked us with his broom while sweeping popcorn from under our feet.

'Stop here!' Neil shouted as we passed a fenced-in city park, and he leapt out and began to run down a narrow gravel path, and all I could do was straighten up the car in the space and run after him. He kept going all the way across the park and around the far side, shouting continually over his shoulder at me to catch up and pointing out how great it was to feel your lungs pumping and your heart racing and cool clean air rushing through your body. I had asthma as a child and, although I have outgrown it, I still am not a natural athlete and easily tire and start to wheeze. This was a fact I explained to Neil when he asked why I had stopped to sit on a bench, but one that he dismissed as a result more of cigarettes than asthma, before dashing off again and leaving me to sit and watch as my tired father used to watch me race around the park many long years ago.

The sun was bright still, but my bench was in the shade of a large building just across the street, and I began to feel the cold. I was too tired to move, though, and just tried to catch my breath as Neil raced round and round. Finally, even he began to tire, and when he got back to my bench he crashed down next to me, putting his arm around my shoulders and letting his head loll back so that he was looking right up at the big blue sky framed by bare winter branches.

'Ah, now there is nothing like some physical activity to make yourself feel alive and well again,' he said between shallow, rasping breaths. 'You've gotta try it, Jack.'

'I tried it,' I said. 'Being on this bench and looking up at the sky works for me.'

'Ah yes,' he said. 'The sky. I remember poor old Andrei Bolkonsky dying on a battlefield and looking up at the big blue sky over Austerlitz, discovering the sheer unutterable beauty of life and the stupid vain futility of the way he had lived his life until then.'

'I thought he got God,' I said flatly. 'Lived a few more disillusioned, purposeless years, let a silly little girl break his heart, and then died.'

'Ah, Jack the cynic,' Neil sighed. 'You can't be a good writer and a cynic at the same time, Jack. Writers are optimists. They leave cynicism to the critics.'

'Or the editors,' I said. 'You should see some of the letters they've written me. I suppose you do have to be an optimist if you expect to get published these days. All the editors at these great publishing houses are just looking for the next Harry Potter. They're not interested in anything serious or literary.'

'They're interested in something that's finished, Jack,' Neil said. 'You can't blame them for the fact that you haven't finished your book.'

'No, but I can blame you,' I shot back.

To my astonishment, Neil looked as if he was about to cry. 'Sorry if I'm getting in the way,' he muttered, taking his arm from around my neck.

'Hey, I didn't mean anything. I was just joking around.'

'Fuck you,' he said, and stalked off across the park, his hands stuffed into the pockets of his tight jacket and his ragged breath steaming out over his shoulder. I sat stunned on the bench for a while, then trotted off after him, catching up soon enough and apologising with all my heart, at which he laughed and said it was OK.

Then we walked around the park for a while, Neil insisting that since I wouldn't run I must at least walk. 'A good old-fashioned constitutional,' he called it. And I, still stinging from his strange tearful reaction and keen to appease him, agreed to the constitutional, and we walked around the park slowly, arm-in-arm, like an elderly couple on the Bognor Regis promenade.

To be honest, I felt a little self-conscious and was relieved there were no people in the park to look and laugh at us. Neil didn't care, or at least pretended not to, and trusted his tongue or his biceps to dig him out of any hole his strange behaviour got him into, but I had no such confidence. It was a relief to me when he breathed out a big 'Aaaahhhh' and said, 'Oh yes, that's better now, my constitution feels truly cleansed. Let's head back now and drive as far as that little Figaro of yours will carry us.' And he strode back to the car, me keeping up with him even though

I felt only slightly rested, and I didn't even really know what my constitution was but it certainly didn't feel cleansed.

As we approached the car, I felt a familiar lurch in my chest as I saw a big piece of paper pinned under the windscreen wiper, its edges flapping slightly in the breeze. I slowed my step, indulging myself for just a little longer in the absurd delusion that it was just a flyer for a local mechanic or pizza parlour. But soon enough the plastic wrapping and the black stamp 'PENALTY' were impossible to avoid. Neil, typically, wanted to tear it up and pretend it had never arrived, but from long experience I knew that they would catch up with me easily enough. 'They take pictures now,' I explained. 'They've got your car there on the yellow line, with the ticket on the windscreen and a time stamp in the corner showing the exact moment of your crime. You can't get out of it.'

'But this isn't a yellow line,' he said. 'It's a parking space. Look.'

'Yep, except Mondays, Tuesdays and Thursdays between twelve and two,' I said. 'It says it on the sign here. I just didn't check properly.'

'Bastards,' Neil muttered. 'Why would they go and do something like that?'

I tried to explain about deterring commuters from parking for the station nearby, but he had no interest. To him it was a Machiavellian scheme concocted by the mysterious 'they' that seemed to shift meanings with every conversation but always existed specifically for the purpose of capturing and subjugating him, Neil Blake. He wasn't able to muster my tired resignation, instead fuming and cursing at the despotic forces behind the ticket, and the camera and everything else that he could think of. I, on the other hand, just accepted the imposition as part of life, something you couldn't fight against, and felt slightly smaller each time. I can't say which is better; they seem to end up in the same place eventually.

Neither of us felt like getting back in the car after that, and since it was after two o'clock we just threw the ticket in the glove compartment, left the car in its now legal space and trudged off into the centre of Aberdeen. We passed a few pubs that depressed us even by their dingy exteriors, generic names and generic middle-aged drinkers at the bar. Finally, on the edge of the well-trafficked shopping district, we came to a place with music booming out of a funky red-lit window with the words 'Bayou Blues' swirling across in blue neon, and we dived right in. Down a few steps and into the dark interior, we were in the middle of the comforting E-flat chords and growling voice of Jimmy Reed. We perched on the edge of the long shiny black bar that faded back into the gloom of the red-sofa interior and ordered two shots of whisky, which we downed in one glorious movement, letting the warm liquid slip softly down, burning our throats.

'What the fuck is this place?' Neil asked the barman, a tanned, thickset, unshaven man in blue jeans and a white t-shirt, who to my relief laughed broadly just as Jimmy Reed shifted over to Bobby Bland.

'This is Bayou Blues,' he said. 'A bit of Louisiana style in the middle of Aberdeen.'

'Well, Aberdeen needs it,' Neil said. 'Either that or a tidal wave.'

The barman laughed again. 'Careful now, that's my home town you're talking about,' he said. 'It may be a shithole, but that's for me to say, not you.'

'You are absolutely right, my friend,' Neil said, nodding as the barman offered us another drink. 'I take it back. I remember this girl I was seeing once and was actually quite serious about. She hated her mother with a passion and used to spend most of our nights together cursing this woman's soulless frigidity that had left her — my girl, I mean — unable to free herself even in adult life to form the kind of deep and intimate emotional and sexual connections that make life truly worthwhile. Well, one night I made the mistake of agreeing with her and saying the woman — her mother, I mean — was a heartless bitch, at which she turned her back on me and went to sleep. I could tell she hated me for saying it, and sure enough in the morning she said maybe we shouldn't see each other any more, which was truly a shame because I was quite serious about her and also I had nowhere else to stay at the time, having just recently experienced an even greater horror with this nurse I was living with ... '

The stories rolled on with the blues and the whisky, and I formed an eager supporting cast along with the barman, who had nothing else to do on that grey Aberdeen afternoon in a Louisiana blues bar with no other customers. The blues ground on over our conversation: Muddy Waters, Freddie Robinson, Howlin' Wolf, T-Bone Walker, Sunnyland Slim. The haze of the whisky, the comforting repetitions of the twelve-bar blues and Neil's stories rolling on to infinity gradually softened us into a meditative mood, and eventually even Neil stopped talking and the barman went back to polishing glasses, while we watched the clean circular motion of his cloth on the glass and listened to the minor chords following in their beautiful twelve-bar progressions, Albert Collins mingling with Otis Rush, Robert Johnson with Pee Wee Crayton.

We listened to the stories of stormy Mondays, crossroads, county jails, hoboes, whisky and women, and in the bawling voices we heard an older, deeper ancestral pain that made a parking ticket seem suddenly trifling. By mid-afternoon we were in need of some rest, and Harry, as the bartender called himself, genially offered us a couple of spots down in the dark back corner. We lay down on the soft red sofas and let Nina Simone sing us a soft blues lullaby, and a few hours later I awoke in dry-mouthed confusion with Harry's hand on my shoulder.

'Sorry, lads, the place is filling up a bit now,' he said. 'People are starting to look.'

'Sure, sure,' I mumbled. 'We'll get out.'

'No, no,' he said. 'Have another round on me. We've got a great band starting in just a few minutes.'

I accepted with a feeling of nausea, and shook Neil awake. Harry was right: the place had filled up now with the five o'clock crowd, and Neil and I stared mistily at the over-caffeinated men and the perfumed, made-up women chatting with false jocularity over their bottled beers. The glasses of whisky stood in front of us, untouched. Soon the band started up, a four-piece collection of pale, gangly youngsters with dark sunglasses and some technically sound but utterly emotionless imitations of well-worn classics by John Lee Hooker. We looked at each other and didn't have to say anything. We shook Harry's hand and said we had to go, doggedly refusing his offers of genuine Louisiana-style crawfish and potato wedges.

For a while we wandered around Aberdeen looking for something to do, but all I wanted to do was sleep and, when I told Neil, he readily agreed. We got a room in an overpriced city centre hotel, leaving our luggage in the car, and jumped straight under the soft sheets of our twin beds, letting their huge, heavy eiderdowns and bedspreads press down on our legs as we watched the evening news and waited an hour or more for our expensive room service food to arrive. I must have fallen asleep with the tray on my lap because I have a vague, uncertain memory of Neil removing it and maternally tucking the sheets in around me before turning out the lights.

7

It felt good to leave grey Aberdeen behind in
the morning, even though we had nowhere to
go. Neil had woken me up before dawn,
jumping on my bed like a child and saying we
absolutely had to get back on the road. He
made coffee on the brown-stained little filter
machine while I showered for the first time
since leaving my mother's house in Crouch
End. We ate a rubbery buffet-style breakfast
in the hotel dining room in stiff, high-backed
wooden chairs with unshaven businessmen
reading their newspapers and looking at us
uncertainly over their bone-hard bacon and
overcooked scrambled eggs.

We headed south, just as pointlessly as the
day before, but somehow it felt different.
Perhaps it was a night's sleep in a bed, or the
fading memory of the embarrassing near-fight
in the café, or the light morning traffic, or the
appearance of the sun in an almost cloudless
spring sky. Whatever the cause, the feeling of
futility had gone. The miles didn't seem
wasted. The road once again comforted us.
The right turns, the zigzags, the crossroads
and farm entrances all slipped by mile after

mile, each individual and yet the same as others we'd seen on this and earlier drives. The familiarity comforted while the novelty intrigued. It was perfect. We didn't speak much; we didn't need to. We just drove and, for an hour or two on those quiet Scottish roads, felt as if we had found what we were looking for.

Near Edinburgh the traffic thickened and slowed. Neil turned the cassette over and soon we were on another mad dash from coast to coast with Sal and Dean, the congested Edinburgh outskirts fading into obscurity next to the vivid colours and huge horizons of the American West. The interminable momentum of the story sustained us through Edinburgh, out the other side and across the border into England. Had we continued it could have carried us all the way back to London, and left us washed up in a bar on the Holloway Road, planning our next trip over a couple of pints of beer and some deafening pop music.

But it didn't happen like that. Somewhere on the motorway, in a flat, featureless landscape of long, slowly waving grass, we came to an absolute halt. People switched off their engines, got out and stood leaning on their open car doors, gazing into the distance. For ten minutes or more, not a single car passed in the other direction. The breeze dropped and the long blades of grass stopped moving. In such a void, even the incantations of Kerouac and the antics of Dean Moriarty could not sustain us long. Besides, the Figaro was in danger of overheating. I switched off the engine, got out and stood leaning on the open car door, gazing like everyone else at the long chain of glinting metal stretching off to the horizon, waiting for something to happen.

Neil sat fuming in the car for a while, then climbed out and started walking up the hard shoulder.

'Where are you going?' I shouted after him.

'I'm walking,' he shouted back. 'See you in York.'

'It's miles!' I shouted after him, but he didn't answer. He stalked on with hunched shoulders and hands stuffed into his pockets, looking down at the tarmac beneath his feet. I kept staring after him, expecting him at least to turn his head and look back, but he seemed to have dismissed me altogether. Neil just shrank into the distance until the road curved a little and he disappeared altogether behind the stationary line of cars and trucks. Still, I leaned on the door and stared into the distance, not wanting to believe that he had gone.

I then felt anger building inside me and I

raised my hand, intending to slam it onto the roof of the Figaro, but the thought of the pain it would bring stopped me, and I just let it fall back onto the open car door instead. I looked around at the other drivers staring blankly ahead, like me. I wanted to get away, but I was trapped. Even to turn around was impossible, as I was blocked in by cars on all sides and by the metal railing dividing our carriageway from the empty lanes on the other side. With some manoeuvring I could probably make my way onto the hard shoulder, but then what? A couple of police cars had already sped past in a flash of blue light, and there were sure to be more. Without doubt, they would catch and ticket me, and I would be banned. A faint breeze stirred my hair for a few seconds, then died.

I don't know how long I stood there leaning on the car door, squinting into the distance, waiting for something to happen. I don't even remember getting back into my car, starting the engine and pulling out onto the hard shoulder. I don't remember if the stalled drivers around me looked at me with envy, admiration or hatred. I don't remember if they cheered me on or called the police on their mobile phones. All I remember is cruising along past a mile of parked cars, with the top down and the wind rushing past me, my heart pounding wildly and my hands shaking on the wheel. When I saw the blue flashing lights up ahead I started to feel sick, and slowed the car. There was no going back, though. I crawled up the hard shoulder, peering ahead to see what was happening and, more importantly, what Neil was doing.

At first, I thought it was an accident. Beyond the almost blinding sea of flashing blue lights I could see a lorry jack-knifed across the carriageway. But then I saw more lorries, and more, and more, stretching out for miles ahead and blocking both sides of the motorway. I began to hear rhythmic chants like ancient battle cries floating over the land. I saw a line of men holding placards and banners, and blowing whistles. I searched for Neil but, just as I thought I saw him, I heard a siren wailing and looked back to see a police car flashing its lights. Feeling as if I was waking from a drug binge to the hard light of morning, I pulled off onto the grass verge and prepared to lose my right to drive. Those few moments of joy as I drove down the hard shoulder seemed distant now and not worth the price. I switched off the engine and waited.

The police car didn't stop. Nor did the one after that, or the four vans that followed. They had more important targets. The vans screeched to a stop and the doors opened to pour out dozens of figures with black batons and riot gear. Encased in their hard black gear, they looked less like men than a swarm of insects. Hard to remember that they were people too, just like the angry truckers facing them now in a line, ready for battle.

Leaving my Figaro marooned in the grass, I walked forward to get a better look. Warnings were being shouted through a megaphone. Acts of Parliament were being invoked. Arrests were being promised. The appearance of fairness, of reason. Disperse now. A chance to avoid arrest.

And if reason failed, as it surely would, then violence would be justified. Protocol would have been followed. The blows of the batons would have legal sanction, while any retaliatory violence would be grounds for prosecution.

The line of truckers held firm, the banners and placards were held high, and there were even some futile attempts to raise a chant loud enough to drown out the voice from the megaphone. I scanned the crowd anxiously and finally I saw him, shouting his heart out and raising his fist in solidarity with the truckers around him.

When I questioned him later he admitted that he didn't really know what the protest was about — something to do with fuel prices, he thought — but I could see it didn't matter to him anyway. 'I just knew it was the right side to be on,' he said. No matter that the previous year he had spent several weeks chained to a tree in protest against the widening of a motorway which would benefit the very truckers he now stood in solidarity with. For Neil such inconvenient inconsistencies did not exist. He was on the side of anybody who raised a shout for something they believed in. The only thing he believed in himself was chaos, for in chaos he saw the only small chance of feeling alive. As he stood there in the line with his lungs bursting and his big fist pumping in the air, the words on the placards above his head were, to him, simply beside the point.

I stood on the sidelines watching as the police moved in. It was all over quickly. Some threw their fists against the riot shields, some ran away, most just waited to be arrested, knowing that this was the real point of all the chanting and banner-waving. If the arrests topped a few dozen they might grab a day of headlines and win for their issue, whatever it was, a momentary pin-prick on the national consciousness. Neil, though, was oblivious to the bigger picture. He fought like a wild animal, punching and kicking against the helmets and armour until finally he disappeared under four or five policemen and emerged a few moments later, bruised, red-faced and handcuffed.

I watched as they led him to the van along with the others. Just before he got there, he noticed me and his eyes brightened. 'Jack!' he shouted. 'You made it!'

Half-a-dozen helmeted heads turned sharply towards me. I looked down at the ground, pretended I hadn't heard, stretched my arms out like a weary driver and walked away. Back in the car, waiting for the lorries to be cleared away and the motorway reopened, I rationalised. Acknowledging Neil would have got me arrested — they were rounding up anyone involved. It would have achieved nothing. In fact, Neil would need me, later, to get him out, to pay his bail money if need be. There was no sense in us both being in jail in some town miles away from the abandoned, unlocked Figaro.

These and a hundred other perfectly sensible explanations swirled in my head. But still the sense of shame would not leave me. I had denied my friend a second time. I thought about just driving home to Crouch End, so impossible did it seem that I would be able to face Neil again. And when, an hour later, I started the engine once more and pulled back out onto the motorway, I was still undecided. But I couldn't avoid going after Neil, any more than the drivers passing the scene of the protest could avoid looking at the police clearing up the remaining debris. There was nothing else for me to do. I was drawn to the police station, to the front desk, to the abusive sergeant refusing to give me information. I could not leave the hot, airless waiting area even as the hours passed and the truckers were gradually released, until it was evening and Neil must have been the last one remaining.

Finally, as the light outside the small window faded altogether and I began to think about finding a hotel room, suddenly a door swung open and Neil stalked out angrily. I got up and was going to speak, but I was afraid of him. His bruises from earlier had swelled to make the left side of his face look monstrous. His eyes and skin burned with rage, and I was shocked by the violence with which the door had smacked into the wall as he pushed through it. I then remembered sharply that I had betrayed him again and my voice died in my throat.

It was too late, though. He saw me, came over and grabbed me by the shoulders. 'Bastard!' he said, shaking me slightly. The grip of his powerful hands was terrifying: he seemed able to crush me if he wanted to. He let me go, though, and, as I started to let out my justifications, he stopped me with a wave of his hand and said, 'Don't worry, Jack, I know why you did it. There was no sense in you getting arrested too, and of course you could never leave your dear Figaro there in the ditch, and so on and so forth et cetera et cetera. Right?'

I said nothing, just looking at him uncertainly.

'But you came here, and you waited for me, and tried your best to get me out. Right?'

'Right.'

'So it's fine. Let's go — where are you parked?'

We walked out into the night and found a bland, chain pub near the car park where I bought Neil a few beers to celebrate his freedom, sticking to Coke myself since I had a feeling we would be driving on somewhere that night. Of course he hadn't forgiven me as easily as he maintained: I could sense his disappointment and resentment as he recounted the day's events a dozen times while telling me I should have joined in. But I was happy to have him free again and to be listening to the stories roll on over the haze of beer in some anonymous pub in an anonymous town far from home. I suspected that he would take his revenge one day, but vowed to myself that I would never betray him again, no matter what he did, and thought that by sticking to this I would perhaps avoid my punishment.

I was right not to drink: Neil decided that we could make it back to the Bayou Blues bar before closing time, order a bottle of bourbon, could sneak it out and spend the night in the car, drinking to dull the pain of his bruises and to erase from his mind the prospect of appearing in court in a few months' time to answer charges of disturbing the peace, resisting arrest, assaulting a police officer and supporting terrorism, all of which could, as his questioners apparently reminded him frequently, put him in jail for a long, long time. Then the next morning we could continue north to the Shetlands as he'd originally planned. 'Going south again was our big mistake, Jack,' he said. 'Once you've started something like this, you can't turn back. The south is rules, order, congestion, everything we're trying to escape from. Going north is the answer, as far north as we can go until we leave behind the colonised world and find a place where we can just be left alone.'

I tried to remind him of what the rig workers had said, but he dismissed them impatiently. 'Stockholm Syndrome, Jack. Identifying with their captors. The whole country's suffering from it. My only mistake was in not going far enough north. We need to keep going north until we can't go any further — it's the only way. We must lose ourselves to find ourselves again. If need be I'll just tramp the icy wastes like Frankenstein's monster, if that's the only place for me. But right now the important thing is to get to Bayou Blues by closing time and get a bottle of sweet bourbon for the road.'

As we drove north to Aberdeen, bits and pieces of his afternoon in custody began to come out. He had been kept so long, he said, because unlike the others, he could not tell them how he had come to be on the road at that time in that place. The truth, that he was a bored car passenger who had gone for a walk and joined in on an impulse, was too implausible.

'They were sure I was an anarchist,' he fumed. 'Which of course I am and I told them so, but not the kind they were thinking of. They wanted to make me part of the 'Black Bloc' — you know, those middle-class kids who hide their guilt under balaclavas — and I tried to explain, very patiently I might add, that no true anarchist would ever join a group. The idea of it is absurd, oxymoronic. And of course then they thought I was calling them moronic, and that's when they got very aggressive and a bit later they slapped on the terrorism charge.'

'Sometimes it's better just to shut your mouth,' I said.

'Like you did?' he asked.

For a few miles after that we were silent, and then, as if nothing had happened, he continued on with his story of what they had said and what he replied. As usual I couldn't tell what was true and what wasn't, but I knew he was in a lot of trouble and desperate to keep talking, moving, drinking and whatever else it took to avoid thinking about going to court and, after that, probably to jail. I wanted to tell him he was stupid, that he had ruined his life for a cause he didn't even understand. But I didn't dare, because I knew he would throw my cowardice back at me, and in any case I was happy just to let him rattle on while the darkness slipped by and the curves of the road gradually helped him to forget.

After an hour Neil insisted on taking over the driving and, after a feeble attempt to remind him that he'd been drinking, I didn't dare to oppose him any more. He immediately slammed on the accelerator and barely took his foot off again, even for red lights and roundabouts. The engine roared, the speedometer surged past seventy and eighty and soon I stopped looking at it, stopped trying to talk sense into him, and just dug my fingers into the tattered old leather of the passenger seat waiting to die.

I'm not sure, even now, if that's what Neil really wanted: the oblivion of a truck or a stone wall in the night. In any case, by some miracle the truck or the stone wall never came. It was late, the road was more or less empty, and the few lone cars travelling along it were lucky enough to avoid us. Neil was possessed by an elemental fury that seemed to make him immortal as he lurched around blind corners on the wrong side of the road, overtook within inches of oncoming cars, and sped through sleeping towns at double the speed limit.

Soon I stopped counting the flashing speed cameras. I knew that I would have enough tickets waiting for me at my mother's house to ban me from driving twice over but, compared to my imminent death, it seemed unimportant. When, at some point, the car suddenly stopped and I opened my eyes to see streetlights and the dark frontage of the Bayou Blues bar, it seemed impossible. I thought for a moment I was having a vision, and wasn't sure if I was dead or alive. Then I leaned out of the window and vomited.

Neil got out of the car and looked in the

window of Bayou Blues. It was long-closed. Even with Neil's furious speeding it had always been an impossible project. It hardly seemed to matter, though; neither of us had the stomach for bourbon. I could barely speak, and Neil's fury seemed to have burned itself out at some point in that manic, suicidal drive. So we just pulled over to the side of the road, turned off the engine, put the seats back and fell asleep.

8

Morning brought new plans. Neil had remembered an open invitation from some woman he had met in a nightclub in Bristol to use an old crofter's cottage in the Outer Hebrides that her family owned as an investment, but never visited. After much fumbling in his bag, he found the crumpled piece of paper with the address on, and we set out to cross over Scotland for the Oban ferry. Neil was excited to have a plan again, and I had no intention of reminding him that we had been intending to lose ourselves in the icy wastes of the mystical north, or that he was facing jail, or that I was almost certainly banned from driving by now. He wanted to forget and I was happy to oblige.

So we left Aberdeen and struck out empty-stomached on a new adventure, suddenly full of anticipation and not caring about the failures that had gone before. We followed the A93, a bland tarmac strip covering endless layers of history. Whereas on most roads you use service stations or major junctions as milestones, on the A93 you measure your progress in castles. First, just

141

off to the right, there's Drum Castle, granted to the Clan Irvine by Robert the Bruce himself. Then a bit further on, just before the town of Banchory, lies the beautiful turreted Crathes Castle, once a formidable fortress in the middle of an impenetrable bog, now a pleasant National Trust garden for old ladies to visit. Swing through forests and glens and picnic spots for another hour or so and you come to Balmoral itself, built by William Drummond, ancestor of the great hero of Culloden, and now summer residence of the family who crushed Drummond and Bonnie Prince Charlie and the hopes of Scotland for another few generations. Ten miles further on, as the misty Cairngorms begin to loom all around, there's Braemar Castle, seat of the Farquharson clan ever since John Farquharson burnt the original one to the ground with the original owner in it. After Braemar the old road becomes a narrow track leading to a dead end high up in the mountains, but the A93, being a modern road, must go somewhere so it curves urgently to the south and speeds on out of the mountains towards Dundee.

We turned off long before Dundee, however, heading due west towards the ancient whisky capital of Oban, out there on the coast, from where Neil assured me there was a ferry to the island of Barra, which he insisted on calling by its original name, Eilean Bharraigh, even though his pronunciation changed radically each time.

Neil was no help with map reading, though, telling me to follow my instinct and the sun, which I did, taking us due west on the B846, and feeling very proud of my navigational abilities, until the road abruptly ended in a cluster of tiny buildings huddled around Rannoch Station — a stop on the remote West Highland Line that winds its way mysteriously off into the hills.

Neil was all for hopping on whatever train came along, but I refused to leave my car in the middle of nowhere, and in any case it looked the kind of station where train departures were measured by the day or the week, not by the minute. So we backtracked for twenty miles along the length of Loch Rannoch and further along the other side. All the way I maintained a hostile silence while Neil gazed happily out of the window, acknowledging no responsibility for the waste of more than an hour's driving time. Finally I found the right road, and we wove through the highlands all afternoon, reaching pretty little Oban around sunset.

Of course there were no more ferries that day, so we found a cheap bed and breakfast in a big old red-brick house on the edge of town. There was only a double room left, but there weren't many other options in town so we took it and, after a few drinks and some bland food in an old-fashioned pub, we went to sleep. In the morning I went out straight after breakfast to check the ferry times while Neil stayed behind to pay the bill.

The morning air was deliciously crisp, and as I walked through the sleepy town I felt strangely free. I wouldn't say that Neil had become an irritation to me, but for one morning at least I was glad to be free of his constant chatter, his urgent needs, his pet theories delivered like sermons from the mountaintop. With a cup of coffee from a local bakery warming my hands and throat, and the salty air clearing my nostrils, I felt as if I could walk forever. Oban, however, is a small town and in just a few minutes I was right in the centre, at the ramshackle old ferry terminal that you can't really imagine serving one island properly, let alone the whole Inner and Outer Hebrides.

We were in luck: there was a departure for Barra at eleven o'clock. I bought a ticket for our car and stood on the dock blowing into my coffee and looking out at the grey, choppy waters. The ferries were small, but in the time I stood on that dock there was a fair amount of activity. Boats came and went, cars were loaded and unloaded with incredible speed. I thought about all the moving parts in each of the ferries and each of the cars, and how many people had been involved in making that little scene possible, from forging the bolts in the ferry's hull, to drawing up the timetable, to putting petrol in the cars at some distant station in the Highlands, or even back in England, and the possibilities soon multiplied beyond comprehension. I started to think about who had delivered the petrol to the service stations, who had drilled for the oil, who had built the car, who had designed the car, who had invented the petrol engine, and so on and on until I realised that if I stood on this dock for long enough I could cover all of human activity across the world both at this moment and throughout history. And I could show how it all was necessary for this one little scene at a remote highland ferry terminal to be playing out as it was. Change one element and you change them all: the cars look different, or they arrive later or earlier, or they are not cars at all but some alternative means of transport that runs on betel juice.

A ferry honked loudly as it pushed out to sea. I looked at my watch. Neil should have joined me half-an-hour ago. I turned away from the ferry and began to walk back to the bed and breakfast, where my Figaro was still parked anyway. But all the way back to the car I still didn't see him coming towards the ferry, as I had expected, and with irritation I stormed into the lobby of the B&B to find him still talking to the landlady in the musty front hall.

'Come on, Neil, we'll be late,' I snapped. 'The ferry leaves in half-an-hour.'

Neil didn't even turn to me. 'I'm sorry for my friend,' he said to the landlady. 'He's a Londoner and not well versed in the ways of treating a lady.'

The landlady smiled in embarrassment and muttered something about it being alright.

'Sorry,' I said. 'I'm a little stressed. Don't want to miss the ferry and be stuck here for another day.'

'Who's stuck, Jack?' Neil said. 'I'm happy here talking to Eileen. We can get the ferry tomorrow.'

'But I've bought tickets.'

'Oh, they'll transfer them to another day for you,' Eileen said in a high, paper-thin voice.

'But we have plans,' I stammered.

Neil came over to me, grabbed my arm sharply and whispered in my ear, 'Come on, Jack, lighten up, would you? Nothing's set in stone, is it? I mean, plans change. Seize the day and all that.'

I looked at him, and the urgency in his face made me wonder what he could suddenly be so keen to stay in Oban for. I looked over at Eileen and saw only a tired, thin, wrinkled woman of about forty whose stringy blonde hair was fading to grey. 'Does she have a daughter, then?' I whispered.

Neil drew away from me, his eyes cold, and it chilled my blood to see how in the second it took him to turn to Eileen his whole expression changed from murderous to genial. 'Can I take you out for a spin, Eileen?' he asked. 'I have a nice little Figaro, perfect for two.'

'That would be lovely,' she said, her face creasing into a thin-lipped smile.

Neil turned back to me, his eyes icy again. 'Don't mind, do you, Jack?' he said, walking towards me as if he meant to cut my throat. I could see now how he survived Feltham Young Offenders Institution and a childhood on the North Peckham housing estate. With his shaved head, crooked nose and teeth, thick neck and bulging muscles and eyes, as soon as the usual amiability and childlike eagerness dropped out of his eyes he became immensely threatening.

'See you later,' he said warmly, half-embracing me in American gangster fashion

147

and using the opportunity to slip the car keys out of my pocket.

'See you later,' I said, and felt like crying as I walked with them to my Figaro and watched them slam the doors on me and head off together to God knew where. I stood on the pavement for several long minutes watching the car get smaller and finally disappear among the traffic.

Suddenly, I felt cold and incredibly tired. All I wanted to do was go to bed, but Eileen was the sole owner of the B&B and had locked it up while she was out. I thought of checking into another place, but the ferry tickets had been surprisingly expensive, and after our night of luxury in Aberdeen my funds were stretched thin.

I trudged into town, sat in a warm café drinking coffee for an hour or so and started to feel better. I even pulled out my notebook and began writing for the first time on our trip. They were just disjointed scenes based on customers in the café and their imagined lives, but the writing felt more real than the lifeless prose sitting on my laptop at home. With the caffeine quickening my blood and my pen scrawling quickly across the page I felt like a real writer again for the first time in a long while. The toot of a ferry reminded me of the expensive tickets in my pocket, and I quickly paid and walked down to the dock, where I found out that tickets were only transferable before the planned departure time. After the boat had sailed, it was too late. I wanted to shout and curse at the man behind the counter, so curt and emotionless was he in informing me that I had just lost seventy pounds. But I have never been good at shouting and it comes so unnaturally to me that my voice soon cracks and begins to sound hysterical.

So I turned away without a word and walked back to the café, where my seat in the window was now taken by a couple of old ladies and I had to settle for a spot in the back, where I sat in front of a blank page for two hours while my mind raced furiously with imagined confrontations with Neil, Eileen and the ticket-office clerk, refusing to be tamed. I had more coffee and a sticky toffee pudding that seemed to have been microwaved straight from a supermarket packet, but my hand still obstinately refused to move across the page, although it now shook a little.

I stayed in the café tormenting myself all afternoon, and then walked back, stopping at a payphone on the way to call my mother. She sounded happy as always to hear from her Jack, but there was an apprehension in her voice as she picked up the phone, and I could tell she was worried I was calling from jail. I reassured her that everything was fine and that Neil was not causing any trouble. We were just having a civilised little road trip and were in Scotland now, a detail which I immediately regretted sharing because she was surprised we had made it so far and started to tell me that I shouldn't drive too fast or go too long without taking breaks. I assured her I didn't, and added that Neil did his share of the driving, and that made her worry even more about insurance issues and so on and so forth. Soon I had to pretend I had run out of coins and quickly put the phone down, feeling guilty and angry at the same time.

My Figaro was parked in the afternoon gloom right outside the B&B, which now seemed to be open, in a spot reserved for staff. I went straight in and saw a white envelope on the hall desk with my name on it. I felt for an absurd moment like a jilted lover seeing a 'Dear John' letter on the mantelpiece, but when I tore it open I found only my car keys and the keys for our room, with a note saying, 'Thanks for the car. Am staying with Eileen. You can stay on in your room for free, she says.'

I walked up the creaking stairs to what had

last night been our room but was now only mine. The big double bed in which we had laughed and joked and eventually fallen asleep together was now neatly tucked in on every side, with a huge floral bedspread over it and a gold-wrapped chocolate left on one pillow.

I sat down and flicked through the five channels on the dusty old TV, finding nothing to watch. There were books on the shelf, mostly well-thumbed detective novels and romances. I picked one up and it occupied a couple of hours, although my ear was always cocked for sounds from neighbouring rooms or, to be honest, one particular sound from one particular room. I thought I heard it once at around Chapter Eighteen of *Confessions of a Baroness*, but it turned out to be just the noise of a television. The crass seductions and telegraphed plot twists began to sicken me, and I skipped about eighty pages towards the end without feeling I had missed anything that a short transition paragraph could not cover.

It was dark outside, but I couldn't sleep. I was hungry, but I couldn't bring myself to go out and find food. I was bored, but going out on my own seemed pathetic. Oban, I imagined, is not a place for singles, in any case. It is a place for happy couples who can sip fine single-malt scotch together in an old-fashioned quiet pub, or have white wine and risotto in a pleasant Italian restaurant before returning to their pleasant hotel for a pleasant bout of lovemaking. Neil had found such a place for himself, but I had not. I felt lonely and alone. I called a couple of friends but they were out or not answering. I couldn't call my mother again, my father was dead, and my remaining relatives would have nothing to say to me other than to ask why I had taken such a strange route to Oban, when I could have just followed the SatNav all the way up the M6. I was alone. Suddenly even dried-up old Eileen seemed preferable to this waking nothingness. I lay awake for hours, staring at the ceiling in profound self-pity, before falling asleep as the birds announced the dawn.

9

To recount the story of the next three weeks would be pointless. Every day involved some aimless wandering around the town, a short bout of constipated writing and an evening of infinite boredom. A few times I tried to go out and meet people, but this merely confirmed my original diagnosis of Oban as a place for people already settled. I barely saw Neil during those three weeks. A few times he came by to borrow the Figaro, and once he even took pity on me and invited me to tag along for the evening with him and Eileen, but he was strangely curt with both of us; Eileen and I had nothing to say to each other, so the experiment was cut short and never repeated.

Finally I could bear it no more and decided to take action. After breakfast, which Eileen cooked faithfully for me every morning as if I were a paying guest, I stayed at my table until Neil shambled in mid-morning for his tea and eggs. He smiled at me and went to sit down at another table.

'We have to talk,' I said.

'Thought you hated clichés, Jack,' he said,

pouring the tea that Eileen had left in the pot for him.

I moved over to sit at his table and looked him in the eye. 'I don't want to stay here forever.'

'Nobody's forcing you, Jack. To be honest I'm amazed you stayed here so long with nothing to do and nobody to do it with. It would have driven me crazy long ago.'

'I want to continue our road trip,' I said petulantly.

'Maybe we will one day, Jack,' Neil said, sipping his tea and looking at me like a faithful old dog he had to put out of its misery.

I looked out of the window at the milky April morning. 'One day?' I said, my voice catching slightly.

'Yes, well, the thing is, what we were looking for all that time. I think I've found it with Eileen.'

'She's old enough to be your mother.'

Neil's eyes hardened again, and I instantly regretted saying it. 'I keep telling you that age is the most ridiculously immaterial and irrelevant thing, Jack. But your stubborn adherence to outdated outmoded ideas of the 'correct' age at which certain people should do certain things only confirms to me that, as they say, you can take the boy out of Crouch

End, but you can't take Crouch End out of the boy.'

I fought with several conflicting responses but, before I could pick one, Neil had started again. 'Eileen may be nothing to you, Jack, but she's a wonderful woman who understands and appreciates me in a way nobody has before. She's warm, she's kind, she loves me and it's as if, even though we're from completely different places and, as you observed, different times, we are made of the same thing. I can start again here, Jack. Clean slate. I haven't used my real name. They'll never find me.'

'Unless I tell them,' I said.

Neil looked up sharply at me, his eyes cold and menacing. In that moment I truly believe he could have gutted me with his butter knife without a second thought. But then his face softened and he said, 'You know you'd never do that, Jack. And besides, what makes you think *you* know my real name?'

A playful smile appeared on Neil's face, then quickly vanished. I sighed and poured myself a cup of his tea, making him shoot me a mournful glance. He was as fond of his little rituals as he was fond of spontaneity in the big decisions of life, and while he could jag around the country at random for years on end, the smallest disruptions to his morning ritual of a pot of tea with soft scrambled eggs on buttered toast could ruin his day.

'Look, Neil, I'm leaving today,' I said.

'Fine,' he said. 'Go back to hide with your mother.'

'And you can stay here hiding with yours.'

His eyes went cold again, and he tapped his knife and fork on the table irritably.

'Look, I'm sorry, Neil,' I said. 'Look, let's just go on to Barra. We can forget all this.'

'No, Jack, we can't travel. Not yet, anyway. Eileen can't leave the B&B without finding someone to look after it first. Since her husband left her she's been all alone here and — '

I put my cup of tea down so hard that Eileen in the kitchen probably worried about her china. 'Look, I wasn't inviting Eileen,' I blurted. 'I'm not going around Barra being a third wheel to you and Miss Perthshire 1974.'

'Fuck you then, Jack.'

'Look, I want us to go together.'

'There is no 'us', Jack. Not after what you just said.'

'Well I'm going. With or without you.'

'Then you're going without me.'

'Fine. I leave tomorrow morning at eleven. If you want to change your mind, you can.'

'Fine.'

After that sorry little exchange, which

needless to say didn't go at all as I had planned, I spent the day mooching around town looking in rain-smeared shop windows and drinking tea behind lace curtains. In the afternoon, after purchasing another over-priced ferry ticket, I consoled myself by buying a fishing rod that my eyes had been drawn to every time I passed that particular shop. I had never fished, but imagined it as the kind of solitary, contemplative endeavour to which I would be constitutionally suited. However, after just ten minutes of sitting on a jetty in the freezing north wind trying not to get my line tangled, I was bored and miserable, and found it impossible to contemplate anything, so conscious was I of amused or wary eyes on my back, seeing me as what I was, a know-nothing city boy trying to be what I was not. I trudged back to the B&B, threw the rod in the back seat with all my other junk, and settled down to an evening of bad TV.

Breakfast the next morning was a horrible mass of confusion and embarrassment. Neil was nowhere, and I guessed that he was waiting for me to be gone before he came down for his tea and soft eggs. I tried to converse with Eileen, but the one thing we had in common was the one thing we didn't want to talk about, and so we bored each other with competing inanities and she retreated to the kitchen at every opportunity.

When it came time to leave I tried to pay her a little for the room, but she would have none of it, saying Neil had already given her enough, at which I blushed like a schoolgirl. She explained that she meant gifts and money, but that only made things more awkward, and I shuffled out of the door into the bright morning with a feeling of death. All the way to the ferry terminal I expected to see Neil on the street with his backpack, waving me down and hopping into the seat beside me, ready to go off to Eilean Bharraigh and raise hell on that small quiet little island. But of course he didn't come.

All the way through the tedious process of queuing in certain designated places and being waved forward an inch at a time by men in fluorescent orange jackets, I glanced to my mirrors or looked up ahead to see if he was boarding as a passenger. I knew he wasn't coming, but I didn't believe it. Even after I left my Figaro on the petrol-choked bottom deck and the ferry chugged out to sea, as I watched the white froth churn up behind us, I expected a thick arm around my shoulder and a deep familiar voice booming festive plans and half-intellectual theories into my ear. But there was only me and the sea; he didn't even come to wave me off.

The ferry chugged and chugged out into the big grey Atlantic until I thought we must soon hit Greenland or Nova Scotia, and I stared out at the flat, unchanging horizon for five hours. I thought of the seventy pounds I'd wasted on a trip to nowhere with no company for no reason. The money my mother had given me was running low, and soon I would have to run back to her with nothing to show for my journey but a few memories of crazy splashing in ice-cold North Sea waves or imagined meetings with ancient Yorkshire tribesmen, a littering fine, a parking ticket, innumerable speeding fines and a fishing rod I didn't know how to use. I hadn't even taken any photos.

Now, after five hours of loud engines, strong winds and the stench of diesel, the gloomy lump of Barra loomed up out of the flat grey ocean. It was late afternoon and the orange-blue cloudless sky provided the best possible backdrop, but still it looked dismal. Barra was a desolate place.

If I had been an ancient explorer I would have passed it by. Its steep hillsides looked utterly barren except for long grasses all bent to one side by the constant chill wind. No habitation, human or otherwise, was visible except for a cluster of miserable grey cottages huddled around the small dock where our ferry slowly pulled in. Without enthusiasm I fetched my car and drove off onto dry land. If it hadn't been for the seventy pounds I had spent on the ticket, I would probably have begged to stay on the boat until it returned to the mainland. As it was, I drove slowly onto the island's only road and followed the scrawled, beer-stained directions that Neil had received from some drunk girl in a sweaty Bristol club.

The island of Barra is only about five miles by seven, but I seemed to bump along the poorly-made road for hours, with big wide tracts of empty grassland on one side and the big grey sea on the other. The road was too narrow and potholed to get up speed, and it had a habit of curving wildly for no reason, or suddenly climbing up a steep incline and plunging down the other side.

My Figaro groaned and moaned in the gathering gloom until, eventually, I saw a small house on the top of a small hill that matched Neil's description: low, painted white, with slate roof and window-frames painted dark green. The gate was easy to unlatch and I drove through. A quick splash up the muddy driveway led me to an area of flattened grass that presumably passed for the front garden. I pulled the Figaro to a welcome grinding halt and sat for a moment doing nothing but watching the grey sea below me, so flat at the horizon and so angry when it whipped the shore.

I wanted to go inside but I didn't want to leave the warmth of the car and go hunting for the front-door key, which was apparently kept behind a loose brick in the side-wall. Once inside, I would probably have to clear off two inches of dust from everything before I could sit down and, in addition, I had not thought to buy food in town, so I would probably have to sup from crusty old pilchard tins priced in shillings.

When I finally mustered the will to step out of the car, the ill wind battered me, almost forcing the car door closed on my dangling leg. Head bowed, I pushed on to the house. The thin paper fluttered in my hand and nearly flew off over the cliff, but I clung on tight to that, if nothing else. I counted twenty-three bricks along from the corner nearest to the sea, and then pulled and prodded at the fifth brick from the bottom, but it didn't move. I retraced my steps and started counting again. Once again I reached the wrong brick, although it was a different one from before. It was almost dark now — I had no torch and had not seen any hotels along the road. The prospect of shivering in my Figaro through a long harsh Hebridean night was terrifying. I had never been somewhere so remote — a Travel Inn or Travelodge was impossible to reach no matter how far I drove. Melodramatic death scenarios swam around in my mind as I fished around in my pocket for a pen and tried with shivering fingers to mark the brick I'd just tried, before going back to the corner and counting again.

The third time I reached yet another brick, two to the left of the one I'd tried before, and felt almost a religious sense of wonder as the brick this time came away in my hand. I reached into the damp, dark hole. There was nothing but sand and spider's webs. I groped around for several desperate minutes, even though the hole was only the size of a brick and the possibilities for hiding a key were limited. I cursed Neil and his ridiculous unplanned plans, and eventually realised my gropings were absurd and stood up straight. I then turned around and saw a woman with wild curly hair carrying a spade aloft like a baseball bat.

'Who are you?' she shouted.

I could hear the naked fear in her voice and it calmed my own. 'I'm Jack Maertens. A friend of Neil Blake? He was invited here.'

The woman let the spade fall. 'Fuck,' she said. 'I almost called my neighbour over. He would have shot you like a grouse before you had a chance to say all that.'

'I'm glad you didn't.'

She smiled. 'I'm Nicola. The girl from the club?'

'Yes, I thought so.'

'Oh, did Neil describe me?'

'No.'

'Oh. Well, come in. It's cold as a witch's tit out here.'

'Right.' I followed her, hesitating for a moment over whether to grab my bags from the Figaro, but decided that it would seem presumptuous.

'Oh, you don't have any bags?' she said in surprise as she let me in.

'I'll get them later,' I said.

'You won't want to. You think it's cold now, you wait until it's been dark a few hours. Even the draught from the window can give you a chill, and that's with double-glazing. Here, I'll help you.'

'It's OK; I travel light.'

Once I was installed in the cottage and had set my bags down in a small back bedroom, I joined her in the living room where she offered me a glass of scotch. It was a very strange room, all bright stripes and faded sixties optimism. A big teak table stood in the centre over a green and orange rug, and the six chairs around it looked fashionably uncomfortable. The two armchairs in which we sat with our scotch, however, were mercifully old and overstuffed. It took some time to straighten out all the little difficulties and misunderstandings over why I was here without Neil, and why she was here when she said she never visited the place, but in doing so we discovered some very interesting things, foremost among them the fact that she, too, was attempting to write a great winding novel, was suffering similar problems to me, and had come to Barra to shut out the world to focus on her writing. I wanted to show her that I wouldn't interfere with her plans so I pretended I was there for the same reason, even though in reality I had no desire to return to that great unwieldy literary gumbo and didn't really know what I would do on Barra without Neil to tell me.

She seemed relieved at this, and to prove my point I went to my room early, leaving her there with her laptop in the enormous old brown armchair. She looked like a true writer, with her legs crossed and the computer resting on top, sending a sickly glow over her rosy cheeks and frizzy red hair.

She even had a special pair of dark-rimmed glasses for looking at the screen. The image of her stayed with me for a long time as I lay in the cold bedroom trying to keep my eyes closed and waiting for sleep.

10

For the next few days I tried to stay out of Nicola's way, going for long walks over the barren hillsides and even visiting what she had called the local beach, a strip of sharp black rocks and pebbles so forbidding that I didn't even get close to the sea's fury.

One day I went wandering off around the island in my Figaro, arriving quickly back at what she called 'town', the dismal collection of dour buildings where the ferry had deposited me. There was a small shop there where I was able to buy some overpriced necessities, and I enjoyed Nicola's gratitude when I returned with them. Every morning when I left she was in the big armchair, legs crossed, and every evening when I returned she was still there, tapping gently. To keep up the pretence I bought a notepad in town and wrote on it at every opportunity, even though my novel was far from my mind and the writing usually consisted of abortive emotional letters to Neil in Oban, alternately begging him to come and telling him I would never see him again. Still, while I was writing I felt I could be in her company without disturbing her, and there was something companionable about spending the long harsh evenings in the warm green and orange room, with her fingers tapping lightly and my pencil scratching on the notepad.

I began to feel more at ease, and stopped going out so much during the day, so that whole days passed in those two comfortable armchairs. But when I was there during the day, I began to feel that Nicola was uncomfortable, and the tapping was not as fluent as it was in the evening.

'I think I should go,' I said over breakfast one morning, when I had been there a week or so. 'I'm distracting you from your work.'

'What work?' she said.

'What?'

She drank a huge gulp of tea and stared out of the steamy kitchen window at the indeterminate sky. 'I've hardly written a word since I got here,' she said miserably. 'I want to, but I just can't. Every time I open up the file, I just stare at the cursor blinking. Then I read over the last paragraph I wrote, and it seems like the most ugly, inelegant piece of writing in the world; I either delete it or spend hours trying to continue but feel that I am building a house in the swamp.'

'Well, that's a good metaphor,' I said. 'You can't be that bad a writer.'

She smiled at me, her plump cheeks crinkling and her brown eyes sparkling warmly; for an instant in that morning light she was truly beautiful. Then it faded and she was just Nicola again, a woman from Bristol that Neil had met in a nightclub.

'You're kind,' she said. 'But you're a real writer. You go for long walks, you get inspiration. Christ, you even write longhand.'

'Letters,' I said. 'I write letters. The thought of touching my novel again makes me sick. I've been working on it for four years now and it's almost entirely worthless.'

She looked at me in astonishment, and indeed I was astonished myself at the unaccustomed honesty. Then she laughed, loud and deep, unashamedly showing the half-chewed toast on her tongue. 'I write emails,' she said. 'Or blog posts.'

'You have a blog?'

She nodded. ''Musings of a Failed Writer'. I write about being unable to write. Get quite a few readers, in fact. I've been doing it for a couple of years now. Must have written a good hundred thousand words by now.'

'A novel.'

'Yep. But a five-hundred-word off-the-cuff blog post is so easy. I can do a couple of hundred of those no problem. But write a novel? I just end up deleting more than I write.'

'Put your coat on,' I said. 'We're going for a drive.'

She blushed a little, and I worried for a moment that I had offended her, but then she smiled that lovely dimpled smile again and asked coyly, 'Can I finish my toast first?'

'If you're quick,' I said, feeling immensely pleased with myself and the success of my sudden new experiment in decisiveness. A few minutes later we were out in the Figaro, coats and hats on, and I put the top down and told Nicola to close her eyes and pretend she was on the Sunset Strip; she laughed and played along, pointing at ramshackle farm-houses saying she could see The Roxy or Whisky a Go Go, or looking at an old weather-beaten farmer saying it was Johnny Depp. I joined in, saying I'd just spotted Paris Hilton when in fact it was a stooped old lady. Nicola loosened her scarf a little so that it flew over her shoulder and flapped glamor-ously in the wind, and then she pulled out a pair of huge, round movie-star sunglasses and put them on. With the bright headscarf covering her frizzy hair and her slightly too full figure hidden beneath bundles of clothes, she looked for all the world like a million-dollar film star.

'Why the hell did you bring sunglasses to the Outer Hebrides?' I shouted over the roar of the engine and the wind.

She laughed. 'I'm an incurable optimist.'

'You'll be a good writer, then,' I said. 'Neil says all good writers are optimists. That's why I'm no good. I'm too cynical.'

Nicola stopped laughing. I instantly regretted saying it. I felt sure that she would start thinking of Neil and wishing that he, not I, were driving her around Barra.

'Neil's an arsehole,' she said. 'Don't listen to him.'

I was too stunned to say anything, and she seemed to take that as tacit agreement.

'I mean, you're a nice guy,' she continued. 'If you listen to him you'll end up feeling inadequate. Neil has a way of making people around him feel like that.'

'I don't need any help from Neil,' I said, with a crooked smile.

'Keep the self-pity,' she said. 'All I'm saying is that ninety per cent of what Neil says is crap, and it's all designed to make him sound great; he forgets all about it as soon as he's said it, but you hold onto it forever, take it all seriously and get screwed up by it.'

I looked ahead. A herd of sheep was crossing the road, forcing me to slow and stop. The sudden quiet was unnatural. 'Why did you invite him here, then?' I said slowly.

'I was drunk and he was charming. I regretted it ever since, and hoped he wouldn't come. Please tell him not to when you see him next. My parents might be up here over the summer, and I just hate the thought of them meeting him. And if I'm here, I know I'll probably fall for that whole act of his all over again, and I really don't want to.'

'Sure,' I said quietly. 'I'll just throw away the directions.'

'No. You keep them. Just don't give them to him.' She looked across at me and smiled with her full red lips in the weak sunlight. I squinted back at her and smiled too, and was going to say something, but then the sheep had moved and we were on the road again.

With the pretence of being great productive writers out of the way, we were happy for a few days. She showed me some hidden spots on the island where she had spent happy times exploring as a child, and we even once ventured onto the beach and splashed happily in the shallow waters as Neil and I had done in the cold John O'Groats' night. But mostly we just stayed at home in that strange green and orange living room and revelled in the warmth and comfort of the huge armchairs.

There was quite a well-stocked bookshelf there. Her father was a great collector of rare first editions even though he had never read a page of them and viewed them only as an investment that, as well as appreciating in value over the years, would also give him bragging rights at dinner parties; while others may have read Hemingway or Dickens, he *owned* them. The happy result was that the books, though old, were in excellent condition. Nicola and I cheerfully worked our way through them, although the thought that the delicate pages in my hand were worth thousands of pounds made me terrified of a careless rip, a splash of coffee or scotch, and I never completely relaxed until the book was finished and back on the shelf in its protective cover.

We didn't talk much or very deeply, but I felt more content in that living room than I had felt for a long time. The novel didn't seem to matter and nor did Neil's absence, and even the road did not seem to be waiting for me anymore. I called my mother in London and asked her to transfer some more money to my account, promising to pay her back by working in a particularly soul-destroying job on my return. She quickly complied so that I had enough to keep making the minimum payments on each of the four credit cards with which I had paid for petrol and food.

The nights were cold in Barra and particularly so in the bedrooms, which had only tiny electric heaters, the antiquated kind that pumped out barely warm air through a loud, power-sucking fan system that would trip the fuse if more than one was used at once. So we had to heat one room first, and then the other, but the result was that one of us would wake up freezing in the middle of the night and have to run through the dead-cold house to fetch the heater from the other's room. Sometimes we solved the problem by staying in the main living room, where the heating was more efficient, just by putting our heads back in those big old armchairs with blankets on top of us and warm scotch inside. But, of course, we would then wake up early the next morning with a horrific deep ache in the neck or shoulder, or with a dead-leg or pins and needles in the arm. So mostly we braved our bedrooms and the cold early-hours run for the heater.

One night, however, I woke in sleepy confusion to find Nicola's cold body pressed up in bed next to me. 'Fuse was blown,' she stuttered, shivering. 'Couldn't face hunting down the torch and fixing it. You don't mind, do you?'

'No,' I said, and so we lay there in the single bed pressed up against each other, with the night getting colder around us, and at some point we began to spoon like lovers, with only two thin t-shirts between us.

In the morning she thanked me and kissed me on the forehead, saying I was a true gentleman, and how nice it was just to be close to somebody and nothing more. I said it was nice for me, too, and after that it seemed silly to spend time and energy heating each room, and worrying about fuses and running back and forth in the night, so we kept the same arrangement and slept deep and long each night, waking happy in the light of day.

11

In the middle of one of our delicious, deep sleeps with rain and wind hurling themselves at the house but not affecting our warm communion, we suddenly woke up to urgent hammering on the front door.

'Who is it?' I whispered.

'Well, I didn't invite anyone over for tea, Jack. Did you?'

'Very funny.'

The noise started up again, clear and distinct from the more muted hammering of rain and wind. 'I'll go,' she said.

'Are you crazy? Could be anyone at this time of night. Let's just ignore it. Stay in bed.'

It was a stupid idea, of course. Anyone who has taken the trouble to find a small farmhouse in the middle of a remote Hebridean island in the early hours of the morning, in a ferocious rainstorm, will not give up. The hammering became more insistent. Then, for a hopeful minute, it stopped, before the silence was broken again by tapping on the window pane.

'It's probably just the wind,' I said. 'Or a

tree branch blowing against the window. It's a gale out there.'

'Let me in, it's cold out here,' came a voice through the window. 'Let me in, Jack.'

'Fuck,' I said.

'It's him,' Nicola said.

'I've got to let him in. You stay here.'

I left the warmth of the bed behind and pulled on my jeans. Neil must have seen some movement through the thin cloth curtains because I could hear him yelping with delight and shouting at me to hurry, hurry before his fingers dropped off.

When I opened the door he tumbled in on top of me in a cloud of cold steamy night air, putting his frozen wet arms around me like some great Arctic explorer back from the Pole.

He could hardly speak at first, and I was overcome with worry on seeing his raw red face and sodden clothes and rigid fingers. In that moment I forgot all about Oban and Eileen and my hatreds and resentments, and even about poor Nicola lying in the warm bed next door waiting for my return. I just manoeuvred Neil into one of the armchairs, pulled the heater as close as I could, poured scotch down his throat and rubbed his fingers and toes back to life. He'd somehow procured a shopping trolley along the way, in

176

which he had deposited all his various dilapidated and now drenched cases and bags, and I pulled that in out of the storm too.

'Ah, Jack, Jack,' he kept saying, at first numbly and hoarsely but with increasing vigour as the scotch and the heat and the motion of my hands began to drive out the deep chill that had taken hold of him.

'You could have died,' I kept saying.

'Ah, yes, yes,' he said eventually, as his chapped lips thawed out enough to form sentences. 'I think I took a wrong turn back there in the town. I was going from memory, you know, the memory of sweet Nicola's words to me that beautiful night long ago, and the memory's not as good as it was before I started pouring drink and drugs and late nights onto it; haw, haw; well as I was saying, Jack, I think I went completely the wrong way around the island, but by the time I realised it was too late to go back and the only thing to do was go forward, forward into the night, always forward, accepting the lashings of the wind and rain as my deserved punishment for the way I treated you, Jack, back there in Oban.'

'It was terrible, truly terrible, and I realised at some point in that long march through the dark that I would only see the house when my punishment was complete. If I'd had to walk three times or forty times round the whole island I would have done it, Jack, and not complained a bit, because I deserved every gust of wind, every drop of rain or seawater or whatever it was that blew into my bones on that long lonely march. But the moon took pity on me first time around and shone on this low white-walled house up on top of the hill, and more importantly on that beautiful little car of yours, its roof glinting beautifully in the sudden shimmering pool of light when all around was darkness and despair.'

'I ran, Jack, ran all the way up the driveway, slipping in the mud in my excitement to see you again, and I paused to kiss the Figaro on the way; yes, Jack, really kissed it, even though the metal was so cold I could quite easily have ended up spending the whole night out there in the freezing rain, with my mouth stuck to the bonnet; haw, haw; but even that, Jack, would have been worth it for the moment when the first warm rays of dawn released me from my torment and allowed me to come to you again and see your big-hearted concern for your friend and brother.'

All this and much more he said in one uninterrupted stream, like a single long holy word, and I sat at his feet rubbing and listening and not caring about the cold or the lateness or the resentments that now seemed so unimportant next to the rapturous fact that he had survived his night out in that lonely hostile wilderness and found me again.

We sat up drinking scotch from the bottle and he told me in detail of everything that had happened with Eileen. 'I was so happy there, Jack, that I just felt I could stay there my whole life and never do anything else, and so I told her exactly that and asked her to marry me right then and there, but she went all scared and said it was too soon. She had just been abandoned by her first husband and couldn't go through all that again and so couldn't we continue as we were and so on and so on, and it became clear to me that she was prepared to let the failures and disappointments of the past rule her present and future; something I cannot stand, Jack, as you well know, because how on earth can you expect your life to get better if you keep on expecting it to be just as it was? It doesn't make sense, Jack, and I told her that, and she replied that I was only saying that because I was young and naïve, and in fact that I was too young for her really and she was too old, and people would think I was marrying her for her money.'

'Well, I flew into a rage for so many reasons

that I couldn't get the words out all at once and so I smashed a china pot of hers for want of anything better to do, and she was so furious with me, Jack, furious in a way I couldn't imagine anyone being furious over a mere pot, a piece of china with a nice little design painted on it, perhaps even a valuable pot, Jack, but nothing compared to the value of a human relationship. So I tried to explain to her that I was just so angry with the idea of conventions and other people's opinions dictating who should marry whom, especially since I didn't even know that she had money and would never have let it influence me even if I did — in fact, to the contrary, knowing she had money made me straight away regret having asked her to marry me, because I knew right then that her money would always be between us as an unwritten unspoken power that she wielded over me, unless I got a job and paid my own way, which, at this point in time, I have no real desire to do unless it is strictly necessary, which it really isn't when I still have another few thousand pounds to go until I hit all my credit card limits.'

'People with money, Jack, are always thinking about it and how to protect it. The money owns them more than they own it, and all I could see for me there in Oban was an ocean of worry stretching off to the horizon.

Was I good enough? Was I making enough money? Would people think I was leeching off her? Would she start to think it herself? I had no interest in all of that, and I told her that everything was ruined, and she cried and asked me to stay with things as they were so warm and lovely and unpressured, but she knew and I knew that things could never revert to how they were. Change one thing and you change everything, Jack. She should have known that at her age, and I told her that too. Then she started crying more and talking about her age again, so I just packed my bags and jumped on the ferry, which quite fortuitously was about to leave just as I arrived at the jetty. That way I could avoid any awkward little scenes or second thoughts, and I just leaped onto the ferry and came here to beautiful old Eilean Bharraigh, stronghold of the ancient Celts, and boy they must have been hardy people to survive in this cold dark windy old place dropped down in the middle of the ocean — can you believe how far it was, Jack, on that ferry? I thought we'd never make it, or that I'd got on the wrong one, or that the captain had got drunk and missed this little rock altogether. Anyway, I'm here now Jack and very glad of it too, for I have so much to say to you and so little time, so little time.'

Suddenly, in the middle of this big long word, he glanced up with a misty look in his eyes. 'Nicola?'

'Hi, Neil.' She was standing in the doorway in a long, soft, velvety brown hooded dressing gown that made her look a little like a monk, but a monk with plump red cheeks, soft lips, wide brown eyes and a mass of frizzy red hair tumbling wildly out and up and left and right.

Neil sat in his armchair and gaped at her. 'My goodness, my goodness,' he said, stroking his jaw. 'I was not expecting to see you here, but what a wonderful moment it is, and it's all perfect, you see, the timing is perfect, and the three of us here will have the best time, the absolute best.'

Then he jumped up, almost knocking me over from my position at his feet, and ran over to hug her, and he even tried to bend down to kiss her. But she pushed him away and said, 'You asked a woman to marry you this morning, Neil. Now you get here and find me, and suddenly you're glad to see me and it's perfect timing because you can just move from one woman to the next? I don't think so.'

She looked at me for a few seconds, then back at Neil, who was standing stunned a couple of feet in front of her. 'I'm going back to bed. It's late. Try not to talk so loud, okay?

I have writing to do in the morning. Trying to finish a novel; that's why I came here.'

'Yes, yes, of course,' Neil said. 'We'll whisper like the grave, my dearest one, and then talk in the morning, when you're not too busy, that is.' And he shuffled back to me, and we whispered for another hour or so before going to bed.

Neil, of course, assumed that Nicola had her own room and that we would share the other one, and I didn't want to tell him the truth because it seemed silly and childlike now for me to have slept with Nicola without doing anything more than hugging. And, also, our innocent nights together felt like a betrayal of Neil, who told me in our whispered hour of conversation how much he had thought about Nicola since Bristol and how much he had secretly burned with hope that she would be there and how crazy he was about her now that he had seen her again, like a vision in the doorway. So he and I went to sleep in the cold second bedroom for a few uncomfortable hours until the sun broke through the thin curtains and we trooped into the kitchen for tea and toast.

'Never again,' Neil said, munching his toast and slurping his tea as he talked. 'I was warmer out there on the road than I was in that bedroom.'

Nicola, who had got up before us and already finished eating, explained about the old-fashioned heaters and the fuses and so on. She looked at me a little cruelly and I thought she was going to explain our sleeping arrangement, but she did not. Apart from that brief glance at me, she was looking out of the window all through the conversation.

Neil wasn't giving up, though. 'Here's an idea!' he said. 'There's a big old fireplace in the living room. I bet we could get it cleared out and ready to use in a day.'

'Firewood is expensive,' Nicola said flatly. 'Especially on an island with no trees. Are you going to pay for it?'

'Ah, that's no problem, no problem at all. I saw a huge store of wood just up the road there, I mean so big that we could easily take a few logs and nobody would ever notice, or mind in the slightest.'

Nicola laughed dryly. 'Theft. You've been here five minutes and you want to steal from my neighbours.'

Neil looked hurt. 'Not theft at all, my dear. Theft implies evil intent and greed of the very worst kind. No, I am simply talking about sharing resources, the very oldest kind of commerce known to man. Sharing wood on a cold night is perfectly natural, perfectly natural. It's crazy to have that big old pile up there doing nothing while we lie here shivering. Besides, as I said very clearly already, we're only taking a few little logs to keep the living room warm. We'll take blankets and sleeping bags and scotch in there and have the warmest night you ever imagined.'

Nicola waved a hand dismissively. 'As I already said very clearly, I'm writing today. You and your friend can do what you like.' She wandered off into the living room, picked up her laptop and took it to her bedroom, slamming the door shut behind her.

'Ah, women, Jack, women,' Neil said jovially. 'All moods and aggravation, but she'll be happy enough when we have that fire roaring, you'll see, you'll see.'

And while I thought of Nicola's contemptuous remark and wanted to say something to stop the tide of Neil's madness, instead I let myself be swept along by it, as usual, and soon had my arm stuck with Neil's up a dusty chimney poking around at decades of accumulated dirt, decay and long-dead gulls. The cleaning took most of the day as we took regular breaks to swig single-malt scotch and admire our progress. Nicola shuffled past from time to time to fetch a cup of tea or a biscuit from the kitchen, but paid absolutely no attention to us unless we addressed her directly and insistently, at which point she would look disdainfully at the fireplace and the spreading soot around it, and shrug. And each time Neil would tell me not to worry and talk about how happy she would be when the fire was roaring, and the scotch and conversation were flowing. He was excited and full of energy, and to look at his flushed face and goofy smile you'd never guess that he'd had his heart broken by a middle-aged B&B owner the day before and was today being coldly ignored by the new love of his life.

Darkness comes early in the Outer Hebrides, even in April, and by the time we had cleaned out the chimney, swept and vacuumed up all the soot and dust from the floor and burned the *Sunday Times* in the grate to make sure that the smoke would disappear, the sun was already sinking to the sea.

'Perfect,' Neil said. 'We'll wait for darkness and then set out. Not that we're doing anything wrong, you understand, but two strangers with a trolley full of wood might arouse undue suspicion among the locals and cause some quite unnecessary and tangential distractions from the main event of getting wood to be warm.'

'Fine, Neil. Fine.'

We drank away a bottle of scotch waiting for all the last tinges of orange to disappear from the sky. By the time Neil said it was time to go, I was cosy and warm in the soft armchair with the scotch burning my chest, and the thought of going out into that cold harsh hostile night to fill a stolen shopping trolley with stolen wood just didn't appeal. I told Neil and for once he didn't cajole, wheedle or whine.

He said 'Fine,' then got up and pulled on his coat and hat with a sad furrowed brow and tight lips, and when I heard the lonely rattle of the shopping trolley disappearing into the night I thought of him alone in the café and alone against the batons and riot shields, and I had no choice but to grab my own coat and run after him.

He was so excited to see me join him in his escapade that he started to run, and I grabbed the handle of the trolley too and ran with him. When the road dipped down we both jumped onto the sides of the trolley and freewheeled all the way down, bouncing over potholes and careening from side to side. The darkness was absolute, so as far as we knew a stone wall or oncoming car could have hit us at any minute, but we were so drunk that it only seemed to add to the excitement.

Eventually we rolled to a stop. The silence

was now so absolute that we realised our trolley ride must have been heard as far away as Oban. We stood still for a minute, listening for approaching footsteps, cars, or the bark of a dog, but there was nothing out there but the distant crashing of waves in the night. We were probably the only living things moving around in all the vast dark miles of sea between Oban and Canada, and the thought sobered me momentarily. We pushed on, the cacophonous rattle starting up again. We said nothing; the noise of the trolley seemed to drown everything out. Then Neil said 'We're here,' and we realised that the trolley hadn't been too loud after all. I saw the huge dark shape of a barn in front of us and felt my way forward until my hands found logs, a wall of logs too vast for me to find more than a small piece of it in that all-encompassing darkness.

'Shit,' I said, feeling a sharp splinter pierce my finger.

'Here,' Neil said, understanding what had happened and feeling my hands until he found the splinter of wood sticking out. He took the finger in his mouth and sucked hard. I could hear his huge jaws working in the darkness, the rush of saliva swirling over my finger, then just as I thought he would pull the skin off, he released me with a big smack of his lips and spat loudly on the floor.

'There,' he whispered. 'Let's go.' I felt my finger and the splinter had indeed gone. I stumbled forward in amazement and started pulling at logs, but they were all stuck fast, weighed down by the massive bulk above them, and the top was too far away for us to reach. If we had managed to dislodge one, it would probably have brought the whole stock rolling down on top of us, and not even Neil could have found a way out of that terrible death.

Fortunately, we stopped exhausted after a while, and Neil suggested searching all around the edge of the pile for loose logs, or at least a point at which the pile was lower for, as he observed, 'That bastard farmer must get them down somehow when he needs them.'

Eventually, we found a spot around the back where the pile had collapsed slightly, and we were able to start loading up the trolley, with our coat sleeves pulled over our hands to avoid more splinters. I pulled the logs off the pile and threw them to Neil, who stacked them in the trolley, and in this way we were able to fill it in just a couple of minutes and begin the walk back to the house.

Uphill it was much slower, and as the exertion of the log-loading wore off we began to notice the terrible penetrating cold. On top of that we had the worry of discovery — or at least I did; Neil didn't seem to care that we had just committed a crime and were now making an extremely slow and noisy getaway. He chattered on about the logs and the tremendous warmth and happiness the fire would give us as we clustered in the living room, the three of us, drinking and laughing our way through the long dark nights. Then he began to talk about how beautiful Nicola was and to reminisce in overwhelming detail about their short time together in Bristol, all of which made me sick with envy. The worst of it was that I couldn't tell who I was envious of and why, so instead I blamed my sickness on the scotch and went off to vomit in a hedgerow while Neil merrily pushed the trolley on up the hill.

12

Nicola was waiting for us when we returned. She seemed to have come to some decision during that day of seclusion in her room, because the sourness was gone and she even helped us get the trolley into the house and wheel it into the living room, not saying a word about the muddy trail it left on her parents' orange and green rug. She watched and laughed and drank scotch with us as we unloaded a few logs and put them in the fireplace, together with a mass of balled-up paper, which Neil lit with a great flourish. For the next half-hour we sat, rapt, on the floor in front of the fire, adding more paper every few minutes as the last set burnt, while those big thick logs remained cold and inert.

When we ran out of paper Neil grabbed a book from the shelf and, before we could stop him, tossed it into the fire. Nicola shrieked, and I dived for it but it was already too hot. By the time I retrieved it, the cover was ruined and the outside of every page charred black. It was a first edition of *To the Lighthouse*. Neil stood there dumb like a child, not understanding what he had done, while I explained the value of Virginia Woolf first editions, lovingly printed by Leonard himself in their Richmond dining room.

'It's the same book as you can get in W.H. Smith for £2.99,' he insisted. 'Same words, same order. Same dull story. Shall we go to the lighthouse? Maybe tomorrow. Et cetera et cetera ad nauseam. All that stuff about Leonard printing it is just hocus pocus designed to make fools part with their money, no offence intended, my dear Nicola, of course.'

I continued berating Neil, but to my astonishment Nicola just drank her scotch and seemed not to care. When I asked her to come to my aid she just shrugged and said, 'It's done now.'

'But it was a Virginia Woolf!' I said.

'It's gone. Nothing we can do.'

'Precisely,' Neil shouted.

'I mean, as long as he doesn't ruin any more . . . '

'Wouldn't dream of it, my dear. I mean, I am most dreadfully sorry about the first one and there's no way it will happen again. And indeed, if there's anything I can do to make it up to you, anything at all, just name it.'

'I'll think about it,' Nicola said, with a coy smile that made my heart shrink. I went out to the kitchen for a while to catch my breath, and when I came back they had found some more paper and were merrily watching it burn while the logs sat dark and cold in the middle.

'Maybe they were wet?' Nicola suggested.

Neil shook his head. 'They're fine. It'll work. They were just cold to the core; they need time to warm up and when they do they'll be fine. Just like you, my dear.'

She laughed and drank more scotch, and they went on like this all evening, trading jokes and laughter and little flirtatious comments, while I sat inert between them like the big shapeless logs on the fire. Eventually I went off to cook dinner, but even from the kitchen every burst of laughter stabbed at me and I was so distracted that I cut my hand while chopping carrots. By the time I got back with two plates of pasta for them, they'd moved the two armchairs over to the fire and were sitting in them happily, watching the smoking paper.

I gave them their food sullenly then brought in my own, which I ate while hunched up on the rug like a dog eating at its master's feet. I think I even made some comment to this effect, and they laughed, but didn't make any effort to accommodate me.

Nicola was now quite drunk. Her brown eyes stared glassily into the fire, her cheeks were flushed and her hair was even wilder than usual. Neil, meanwhile, chomped away loudly and happily, saying every once in a while that the logs would catch any minute, and we just had to be patient.

He was right. After another bottle of scotch and some increasingly disconnected conversation, we stared in amazement and then whooped in delight as the logs began to glow red. Neil was in the middle of a long self-congratulatory speech when suddenly a loud crack interrupted him, and the fire spat a lump of molten wood angrily across the room, where it lay burning a hole in the green and orange rug. Neil ran across and stamped it out with his bare heel, the scotch anaesthetising him until he had completed the operation, after which the pain suddenly hit him and he yowled like a dog on heat.

By that time another lump of fire had cracked out of the grate, and another, and another, and soon the living room was a fireworks display and the orange and green rug was ruined. There was nothing we could do except pull the armchairs out of harm's way, drag the smouldering rug off into the kitchen and douse it in water, and then cower in a far corner of the living room watching the red glowing lumps of fire spinning out into the room and dancing across the bare hardwood floor.

'It's punishment,' Neil whispered.

Nicola laughed. 'It's chestnut. They use it around here to heat their boilers. I should have realised that's what it was.'

We jumped back again, as a glowing chunk of wood almost reached our feet. 'No, it's punishment,' Neil said solemnly. 'I made a vow after my last time in that horrific soulless borstal that I would never again be caged up behind bars like a lion in a zoo. Since that day, I have curbed my natural instinct for crime, which was never really anything more than a desire for some subversive fun, and avoided anything which might possibly be construed by this repressed, authoritarian world as a crime.'

'Ah, so you admit now that stealing wood is a crime,' Nicola said, laughing.

'I was talking about the little incident on the motorway,' he said, glancing at me. 'But yes, the wood, too. A crime against a fellow crofter. I admit it and repent,' Neil said, so seriously that both of us laughed at his drunken delusions. But he kept on about his punishment at the hands of one of life's essential elements, after only the night before he had almost died at the hands of the cold north wind, and wouldn't be persuaded that we had simply used the wrong type of wood.

Finally, Nicola said we were all too drunk to make any sense and it was time to sleep, and the two of us gathered up blankets, sheets and pillows from the bedroom while Neil crouched shivering in the roasting living room, mumbling what sounded like drunken prayers under his ragged breath. We laid out the bedding into one big pile in the furthest corner of the room from the fire, which was now blazing with an infernal heat that warmed the whole house and seared anyone who stepped too close. Shielding our faces with our arms, Neil and I carefully threw a couple more logs on to last us through the night, and retreated to our bed in the corner, where the scotch and the warmth quickly led me from consciousness.

At some point I woke in the darkness, dry-mouthed and with a fierce pounding in my head. It was becoming too familiar a way to start the day, and I always vowed in those moments not to drink again. But then the evenings rolled by full of light and warmth and laughter, and I just wanted to live and be merry, and the cold shivering pain of morning was far enough away for me to consider it a price worth paying. This morning, it was worse than ever and on top of everything I was bitterly cold, the fire having angrily burnt itself out. I hurried over, blankets wrapped around me, my breath steaming and my bare feet brushing against lumps of ash on the floor, and threw several logs and some paper onto the still-warm embers.

I sat close to it as the paper flamed and smoked, greedily drinking in the warmth that caressed my ice-cold face. After a few minutes, though, I realised something was wrong. I had stumbled over no bodies when I got up. I had heard no snoring and, in some strange way beyond description, I knew that the room I was sitting in was empty of other human life. I was alone. Once again, as in Oban, I strained for sounds of Neil, but could hear none.

I didn't need to. I knew what they were doing, or had done, and the thought of it made me sick. From being too cold I suddenly felt too hot, and rushed over to throw open the window and let my head hang limply out in the damp dark night. When the nausea had passed and I raised my head, I could see streaks of orange over the sea. Gulls called out into the gloom, and somewhere a crow squawked. I resolved to leave. Once again, everything felt broken. The thought of speeding along on an open road with the image of Neil and Nicola receding in the rear-view mirror calmed me like a cool ointment on a fevered forehead. I had to go, and this time I would not look back. I would find my own flat in London, get a job, pay my own bills for once and stay up late into the night writing my novel with a pot of coffee by my side and Beethoven blasting out of my stereo. My life would be heroic, full of noise and fury and delights of its own, not a sad shambling existence following around after others, envying their ability to live and sucking from their spontaneity like a leech.

I turned quickly around and Neil was standing there like a ghost, quiet and pale in the early morning gloom. 'We must leave right away,' he said. 'Something terrible has happened.'

'What?' I asked, but he waved me away and said he would explain everything in the car.

'Where's Nicola?' I asked.

'In her room,' he said, but would say no more, and I wanted to grab him by the shoulders and say something forceful and decisive that would change our lives forever, but could not muster the energy in my sick body and just staggered around gathering my things and throwing them in a bag. Neil's entrance and plan had caught me completely on the wrong foot and I could find no way of telling him that I wanted to go on my own. Besides, as he was clearly upset and shocked I could not leave him there on his own. I could jettison him in Oban, or in Glasgow, but not on a tiny island where he had almost died once trying to find me and would probably die this time trying to walk back to the boat, so plaguing me with guilt for the rest of my life.

We were soon ready, and I wanted to say goodbye to Nicola, but he said, 'She's sleeping.' I insisted that she would want to say goodbye to me and he insisted more forcefully that she would not. For a moment I thought about pushing past him and going to Nicola, at least to see if she was alright before we left, but he took a menacing step forward and the sheer bulk of his broad chest and muscular arms seemed to make him impassable.

I reversed back down the muddy track with the sun casting its grey light on the little white house with its green window frames. Only two mornings earlier I had been planning to stay in that house with Nicola for as long as she would have me, and now Neil had burst in, a great cloud of confused but boundless energy, and everything had changed. We bounced back over the potholes with the top down and the chill wind lashing our heads — best hangover cure, Neil insisted, and of course he was right. Along the way Neil kept his promise and told me everything that had happened that night, most of which I had already guessed in that sick, lonely moment in front of the fire. The only part that was new to me was his description of Nicola's sudden coldness in the morning, her insistence that he and I leave immediately. 'She wouldn't listen,' Neil cried. 'She was warm and then cold like the grave. She just wouldn't listen to anything I said.'

I thought of Nicola waking with that same sickness in her stomach, that same dryness in her mouth, the same feeling that everything in the world was grey and empty, but with the added insult of seeing a man she hated lying next to her basking in the satisfied warmth that coats a man after sex. Who knows, he might even have tried to penetrate her resistant body again that morning, because he had confided in me on many occasions that he liked nothing better than morning sex, when the woman is either asleep or half-asleep and doesn't know at first whether she's dreaming or not. I could feel her anger, mingled with the shame of having let Neil and scotch charm her into doing what she didn't want to do, but knew all along she probably would. And I sympathised with her, for here was I driving along with the man I had only half an hour earlier vowed to expunge from my life.

For mortals such as Nicola and me, resisting Neil's will seemed as futile as resisting the rush of the tide or the force of the wind. He had swept me along for as long as I had known him, and he had done the same with Nicola, and she had fought back in the only way possible, by getting him out of her life. I wanted to do the same, but I knew that whenever he was gone I felt lifeless and empty, as I did for those few weeks with my relatives over Christmas, or the deep doldrums of my time in Oban drifting aimlessly from café to café with nothing to do and no idea of where my life would go without Neil leading it. Nicola would be feeling that way now as she pottered around the cold house (the logs I threw on had not ignited). She would be glad to be rid of Neil and yet be listening all the time for the sound of our Figaro puttering up the muddy path. She would do the dishes and see him eating, would make the bed and smell his musk on the sheets, would attempt to relight the fire and hear his mournful, ridiculous drunken talk of punishment. I knew.

We arrived at the ferry terminal with an hour to spare until the morning boat departed, and sat on the dock watching the grey sea wash in. We left the car engine on with the scratchy speakers booming out the last sad chapters of On the Road. Everything was going to hell in a Mexican brothel. Dean and Sal seemed to have taken a wrong turn somewhere a long way back, and there was no chance for them to find their way again. Even Matt Dillon sounded as if he had hit rock bottom. Soon Sal was in a fever and looked up to see Dean with his trunk packed, abandoning him and heading back over the border. I felt the same anger as I had years ago as a teenager, reading the book in my bedroom when I should have been asleep. For all my desire to be Dean Moriarty, it was always poor shambling Sal Paradise that I felt sorry for, even as his long-suffering decency sickened me. I hated Dean for leaving and I hated myself for caring.

I looked across at Neil. He was looking out to sea and not seeming to hear anything, but he must have been feeling uncomfortable too because he stood up abruptly, walked over to the Figaro and turned the keys to silence the tape.

We were silent for a while, with just the sound of the sea lashing a little half-heartedly at the shore. Then Neil started up another long riff on infinity, one I felt I had heard before in another place and time. I told him so, and he said irritably that it was impossible because he'd only recently started thinking about the concept himself.

'It was in Oban with Eileen,' he said, 'Reading a wonderful little story by this clever Argentinean writer in which a man's grandfather or great grandfather or something has written this amazing novel in which every possible outcome is narrated, not only the one that happened to come true. Or perhaps they are all true, and we are only aware of one of them. For instance, perhaps there's another reality in which I get married to Nicola and we live happily ever after in that cottage, or another in which you get together with Nicola yourself, or another in which you and I do, or still another in which we never meet. You see? This novel included all of them, and with each forking path the number of possibilities increased exponentially until soon the novel became incomprehensible and everyone in his family thought he was mad, until generations later in the middle of a war this wise old academic explains it all. But then the grandson has to kill him immediately for various intricate reasons of plot which it wouldn't make sense to go into. But I've been thinking since then that this novel, the novel of all outcomes, is really the only novel to write. Everything else now seems so monotonous. Cause and effect, cause and effect. Everyone's writing the same stories over and over and just changing the names of the characters. You should write it, Jack. Ditch that one that's bogging you down. No offence, but it's probably worthless anyway. Sit down and write this novel that describes all the outcomes of every event and every outcome of every outcome. Break out of one dimension, Jack. It's the most important task of our time.'

'It's impossible,' I said. 'If you took it to its logical conclusion it would contain everything. It would be infinite. Even to understand it, let alone write it, you'd have to be God.'

'Exactly,' Neil said, staring out to sea. 'Infinity, Jack, infinity, that's really it. Be like God, Jack.'

He said it as if it was a task, like driving onto the boat or eating a sandwich. In that moment I thought of what Nicola had said of him, and realised that it was true. He was no great mystic. He just said things for effect, even if they were meaningless. My head started to pound again.

'The boat's here,' I said. 'Let's get on.'

We walked away from the dock, and I kicked a stone across the empty car park. Only a couple of other cars were waiting to board the ferry. 'Here,' I said, handing Neil his ticket. 'You get on, and I'll join you. I've got to go and get petrol.'

'Ah, get some in Oban,' he said. 'It'll be cheaper there.'

'I don't want to risk it. I'm really low. Besides, why waste time in Oban? I've got ten minutes here. I'll fill up, and then in Oban we can just drive straight to a bar, or on to the open road and feel the wind in our faces again.'

He smiled. 'OK, Jack.'

I jumped in and started the car, watching him slouch his way to the ferry. When I was a child I had watched a film in which a man abandoned his faithful dog on a beach and drove away, leaving it to wait there for him all day and all night with its big mournful eyes, and the sad music had made me bawl. Driving away and looking in the rear-view mirror I felt like that man. I imagined Neil waiting faithfully on the boat for me to return, and felt the childhood tears return to my eyes with the force of two decades' imprisonment.

At the top of a hill above the town I pulled over and got out to clear my head. I looked back at the ferry and the black dot on the top deck that I fancied was Neil. I felt a great pang in my heart, and jumped straight back in the car and sped down the hill. The ferry was getting ready to leave, but a man on the dock in a fluorescent orange jacket waved his hand to signal them to wait. I drove up to the ramp.

'You're lucky,' said the man. 'We were about to go.'

'Thanks,' I said, and showed my ticket.

Up on the top deck Neil waved at me. 'I thought you weren't coming!' he shouted. 'Thought you were going to go and ball Nicola yourself, haw haw.' And he made a whole range of obscene gestures up there on the horizon, gyrating against the rail and shouting and laughing.

The man in the fluorescent orange jacket looked at me. 'Well, are you going on board then? We've got to leave now.'

I looked back at him. 'I don't know,' I said.

He grimaced in frustration. 'Well, we can't wait for you to make up your mind, son.' He gave me a few seconds to speak before signalling to a colleague on deck to raise the ramp, and he jumped on as it lifted up and away from me.

Neil stopped his gyrating and stared at me. His face was not angry, or even surprised. He just stared at me, with interest. He said nothing. Neither did I. I stared back as the boat's engines roared and churned froth in the sea and the big lumbering ferry moved slowly away. All the while Neil looked at me and I sat in my Figaro looking at him getting smaller and smaller until all I could see was the shape of the boat, then just a dot, then just the sea.

13

Nicola was not surprised to see me return, but she was surprised that Neil was not with me.

'What did you do, push him in the sea?' she asked, holding the door half-open.

'I put him on the ferry,' I said. 'I had to come back.'

She ran a hand through her frizzy hair and stared into the pale morning sun. 'Look, there's nothing to come back to, Jack. I suppose you think that because of last night I'm easy and you can come and get some for yourself, after being all celibate and gentlemanly all those nights. Well, sorry but no. I was drunk, that's all. It was a mistake.'

'I know,' I said. 'I just came back because I realised I wanted to go back to how it was before he came. I haven't felt like that for a long time. And I've still got a whole shelf of first editions to get through.'

She smiled a little. 'Perhaps,' she said, and opened the door, and I went in. We had tea and sat in the armchairs reading our books all day. The living room looked very different without the big orange and green rug, which

Nicola said she had disposed of that morning. She'd cleaned up the ashes as well, but the burn marks in the floor were a permanent reminder of Neil's ill-fated idea. The big black scars sat between us, and our eyes would sometimes stray to them as we read. Halfway through the afternoon, Nicola put her book down and took a bottle of scotch from the kitchen with two glasses. 'Think I need to relax,' she said.

'Me too,' I said. We drank the scotch for the rest of the afternoon, listened to Radio Three and stared into the empty blackened fireplace. A couple of days passed like that, with the scotch coming out earlier each day. At night we curled up in bed together like before, but just as I was falling asleep she would stretch and wake me up, and later on I did the same to her. We complained at each other but kept clinging on through the cold sleepless nights, both of us, I suspect, secretly waiting for a tap on the window.

On the third day, we tried going out for a drive to avoid hitting the scotch straight after breakfast. I put the top down again, but Nicola complained about the cold and I had to agree that even with coats and hats on it was quite uncomfortable, so I pulled over and put it back up. We drove all around the island, saying little, but remarking every now and then on a beautiful old church or spectacular windswept Atlantic vista. We arrived back at town faster than I expected, and took the opportunity to stock up with bread, butter, scotch and other essentials. I filled up with petrol; we watched the morning boat depart for Oban. There was nothing else to do after that but go back to the house. I wanted to take the long way, but Nicola said why go back the way we had come when it was twice as long? I shrugged and took the short route, and we were soon home again. We tried to read, but again found we couldn't focus, so we brought out the scotch and put on Radio Three.

We made pasta for dinner and sat eating it at the kitchen table like a long-married couple, our knives and forks scraping the plates loudly and our conversation confined to passing the parmesan and complimenting each other on the cooking (I'd done the pasta, she'd done the sauce). For the first time in a long time, I missed my mother's television set. I thought of her sitting in front of it watching Agatha Christie dramas or doing her crossword, and I wished I could be there helping her with the odd clue, instead of out here in the middle of nowhere in a cold draughty house with nothing to say.

We had wine with dinner, a coarse Italian

white that Nicola said she liked. I politely mumbled my agreement. We had ice cream for dessert. It was the old-fashioned three-striped Neapolitan kind that used to pass for exotic before Ben & Jerry hit town. It reminded me of my childhood again and I felt a pang. Until that night I had not felt myself to be on an island. I had known I was, but I had not felt it. Now I felt it, and I felt it to be the smallest little rock in the widest ocean. To get back to Crouch End from here would take days. I thought of Donna's Kebabs, the Dog's Head, the old men's pubs with the dogs dozing underfoot. I thought of the dark drizzle on the Holloway Road, the double-decker buses roaring past isolated gaggles of drunks, the long stretches of darkness between the bright lights of a pub, a chicken shack, a burger joint. I smiled at Nicola and offered to do the washing up. She smiled and said she would dry. We took a long time over it, and by the time we got back to the scarred floor of the living room it seemed pointless to do anything. The cold was already setting in, regardless of the heaters. We went to bed.

That night I was colder and lonelier than ever before and clung tight to Nicola, burying my face in her neck. Her skin was so soft and smooth, and smelled sweet, and some long-dormant memories awakened in me and

I began to kiss her neck ever so softly, to which she responded by sighing deeply and slowly turning around to face me in the darkness.

I felt her lips on mine, her hand reaching up under my t-shirt and the smooth inside of her leg rubbing the rough, hairy outside of mine. For a few minutes we kissed gently like this in the darkness and I forgot about Neil and my novel and the failures that bogged me down and I achieved the perfect weightless glory of living free of the past and future.

Then I rolled Nicola over onto her back and her face fell into a shaft of moonlight from the window and the dream was broken. I saw her flushed face and thought of Neil's muscular body pounding away on top of her, his broad face sweating, large veins pulsing in his shaven head.

'I'm sorry, Nicola,' I said. 'My heart's not in it.'

I pulled away from her and she smiled sadly. 'I'm not what you wanted,' she said.

'It's just all wrong. I'm sorry, Nicola,' I said quietly. 'I can't do it. I'm sorry.'

I got out of bed, got dressed, piled my things into the Figaro and drove it straight up to the edge of a cliff where I sat shivering in the darkness waiting for the sun to rise over the sea. Clouds had massed on the horizon and the sunrise was hazy and hidden. I dozed off for an hour or two around dawn and had to speed down to the town to catch the morning ferry back to Oban.

Being out on the wide-open sea did nothing for the aching emptiness I felt swallowing me from inside. I stood on the top deck where Neil had stood three days earlier, leaning over the rail. I looked out at the flatness stretching from here to the North Pole and tried to feel inspired, but I felt nothing at all. I suspected I would never feel anything again. An old man tried to talk to me as he smoked his cigarette, but I didn't have the energy to reply, and he soon retreated to the warmth of the seating area inside, leaving me clinging to the rail, battered by the wind. I tried to think about what I would do on the mainland, but it was hopeless to pretend. I knew. It was the one thing I didn't want to think about and yet I knew that all the other scenarios of independent paths and bold new courses were base self-deception. I knew.

As soon as the mainland came into view I went back down to sit in my car. I had forgotten how craggy the Scottish coast is and from the first sight of land it was almost an hour before the boat finally came to rest in Oban. By that time I had smoked my way through half a pack of Marlboros, keeping the windows shut so that nobody saw the smoke billowing from my car, in contravention of the rules. The build-up inside made my eyes water and wound my nerves even tighter.

As soon as the ramp was down I honked impatiently and inched forward to graze the bumper of the car in front. The men in fluorescent orange jackets tried to halt me and let the other line go first, but I ignored them and pressed on through their shouted protests. Every traffic light and zebra crossing in Oban oppressed me and I felt immediately hemmed in after the wild openness of Barra. Getting to Eileen's B&B seemed to take hours, although it could only have been five or ten minutes. I was the worst kind of driver, slamming my foot impatiently from brake to accelerator, accelerator to brake. The genteel folk of Oban shot me nasty or concerned looks, but I didn't care. I just pressed on through the afternoon traffic until Eileen's shabby old red-brick B&B came into view and I screeched up to the front door and jerked on the handbrake in an illegal parking spot. I jumped out, keeping myself to a walking pace only with great effort.

'He was here, Jack,' Eileen said, as she opened the door, looking paler and older and more ghostlike than ever — almost transparent as she stood there on the doorstep in the watery afternoon sunshine.

'Where is he?'

'He was waiting for you, I think, even though he pretended he was here to make things up with me. He stayed a few days but his eye was always on the window or the phone and he spoke of nothing but you and your Figaro and how you'd got separated when you went for petrol and didn't make it back to the boat in time. 'He'll be here soon,' he kept saying. 'On the next boat, the next boat.' In the end I told him to leave. I couldn't stand it any more. He left earlier this afternoon.'

I took an impatient step forward. 'Where did he go?'

She stepped back warily, her hand gripping the door as if ready to slam it. 'I don't know. He just left. Said he was going south.'

'South?' I said. 'South where? South as in Glasgow? London? Cornwall?'

'Just south, Jack,' she said with a tired sigh. 'He just said it was time for him to go south. Said he'd hitch a ride somewhere.'

'Hitch?' I said, a little hysterically. 'You let him hitch?'

She closed the door a little on me. 'I'm not his mother, Jack, no matter what you might think. I can't control what crazy thing he does next.'

'But hitching? Nobody hitches these days. Nobody picks up hitchhikers either, unless they want to kill them and eat their spleens for dinner.'

Eileen shrugged, and was starting to look a little scared of me. 'Then go and find him,' she said. 'Or leave him to it and forget him. I can't do anything else.' With this, she closed the door.

If I was impatient before, I was truly driving with a fury now, beeping and fighting my way through Oban's narrow streets. The sky was darkening. A light rain started, and quickly became heavier. I fought my way onto the main road out of Oban, the A85, on which we had arrived long weeks ago in bright spring sunshine, after touring past castles and lochs. Now it was a dour muddy road slick with rain and clogged with cars and lorries leaving Oban for obscure spots in the highlands or the long trek south to the lights of Glasgow and Edinburgh. I scoured the sides of the road but could see nobody.

I drove frenetically all thirty miles of that busy road heading east through the dark louring mountains to Crianlarich, a natural hitching point because it's where the road joins up with the big wide A82 heading south

216

past vast Loch Lomond to the dormant cranes of the dying Clydebank shipyards. The sun had almost completely gone now and the rain was hard. I splashed frantically up and down the A82 in both directions, looking all around that junction for a forlorn sodden figure with his thumb out, but found nobody.

I pulled over, turned off the engine, and put my head on the wheel. Suddenly I felt tired and old. The energy of that mad impatient drive had burned itself out, and I now felt barren and hopeless. I pulled out my tattered atlas and looked at the possibilities. If Neil had found a ride south to Glasgow, then he was gone forever. The only thing to do was return to my mother in London, waiting for a knock on the door that would probably never come, or hang around sadly in old haunts on the Holloway Road hoping for that thick arm to drape itself around my shoulder and that big booming voice to fill my life again with silly stories and mad theories, and festive plans for nonsensical adventures.

With my finger I traced the road all the way back to Oban, looking at all the side roads. There was no other way he would have gone. But then, at Oban, I saw a thin little red line snaking out to the south. It was a dead end, I knew. It ran south for a good fifty miles, but down a big peninsula at the end of which you had no choice but to turn around again, or wait for a ferry to put you back on the landward side of the Firth of Clyde. Neil wouldn't know this, though. He scorned maps and planning of all kinds, preferring to trust his instincts and the stars. He would have wanted to go south, so there was a good chance he would have started out on that long southward road with his thumb out, hoping for a ride to Glasgow and with no idea that he was heading down a fifty-mile cul-de-sac.

I cursed myself for driving all the way to Crianlarich without checking this possibility back in Oban. There was nothing to do now but wheel the Figaro around and drive west to the sea. If I didn't check, I would always wonder whether he had been out there waiting for me to pick him up and had realised slowly as the sun set on that dark lonely road that I wouldn't come, just as I didn't drive forward onto the ramp of the ferry back in Barra.

I drove like a madman all the way back to Oban, driving as Neil had driven that night heading for John O'Groats, with my hands gripping the wheel and my bumper inches away from the car in front, always impatiently nosing out over the centre line to look for a passing opportunity. The traffic was lighter on the way back as the evening turned to night, and I made better time. Once, close to Oban, a speed camera flashed as I drove over the little white lines in the road, but it didn't seem to matter anymore. I thought only of Neil on the road with his thumb out in the downpour, and pressed harder on the accelerator, the Figaro whining in protest but driving forward through the rain with everything its little one-litre engine could give.

The streets of Oban were emptier now and I quickly blew through town and out the other side onto that little road winding down the coast to nowhere. I drove for mile after mile through the darkness, caught forever between the desire for speed and the need to keep my eyes on the sides of the road. Neil, after all, might have given up on a ride and be sheltering for a while in the shade of a tree, or have stopped to rest, or do up his shoelace. Or he might have realised his mistake and crossed to the other side of the road to get a ride back to Oban.

I couldn't afford to miss him. So I drove awkwardly, hunched over the wheel, looking from side to side, ramming the accelerator and then tapping the brake, lurching forward and then skidding slower. The road was empty. If Neil was out here, he had no chance of a ride. At one point on that lonely coast road I thought I saw him, but as I sped closer I saw that my headlights had merely fallen on an old road sign covered with a black tarpaulin. At that moment I felt desolate, convinced that Neil had slipped out of my grasp forever.

Then, a bit further up the road, I saw a hunched figure, stumbling forward like an old pilgrim in the cold and rain, with bags lumped on his back. I pulled over and rolled down the window, and the man's face bent to peer in. Beneath the hood of the coat I could see those familiar broad, thick features, the mouth spreading into a weary grin as he said, 'Jack. I knew you'd come.'

'Get in!' I shouted. 'You'll die out there.'

Neil rubbed his chin slowly, as if we were still sitting in front of a roaring fire swilling scotch instead of out here in the dark cold rain, clinging to the edge of a continent.

'Yes, well, here's the thing, Jack,' he said slowly. 'I realised that driving around and driving around and driving around is the most pointless thing in the world. We have to hitch. Hitching is the thing, Jack. That's living, that's experiencing life on the edge, not knowing from one minute to the next where you're going or why you're going there.'

'Shut up and get in, Neil!' I shouted into the rain and wind, but he was oblivious.

'You'll have noticed Jack that, in the first half of On The Road, Sal and Dean are hitching all over America and meeting lots of wonderful new characters all of the time. Then in the second half they hardly meet anyone. It's the same stale round of girls and friends. Just Sal and Dean and Camille, and in the end even dull old Remi Boncoeur, whom we left in San Francisco in Part One and were happy to think we'd never see again. It becomes circular, Jack, and stale and static, and they lose interest and give up, and let themselves be beat. But it doesn't have to be that way, Jack. If you keep on moving, you can beat it. You can win. You can live.'

I turned off the engine and got out of the car, marching around to face Neil. 'This road doesn't go anywhere,' I said.

'Ah, now that's your mistake, Jack. You always have to be going somewhere. Who said I had anywhere to go?'

'But it's a dead end, Neil, like that road we took in the Highlands where we had to turn back around again. It reaches the end of a peninsula and then there's nowhere to go.'

'Well, then I'll see what the end of a peninsula looks like,' Neil said stubbornly. 'I've never seen that before. Sounds as if it could be interesting.'

I sighed, and gave in. 'OK, Neil, I'll take you to the end of the peninsula. You can hitch a ride with me all the way there, and then we'll turn around and go back again.'

He shook his head. 'Doesn't work that way. That's not hitching. It's tourism. That's the problem with what we've been doing up to now. We've been stuck in this car of yours all by ourselves, listening to someone else's fairytale and not really living life ourselves. Out here on the road by myself, Jack, walking on to see what's over the brow of the next hill, with nothing but the tarmac beneath my feet and the trees and hills on either side and raw nature all around me, I can't tell you what it's been like. I'm starting to understand things, Jack. You must join me. Ditch the Figaro here and walk on with me, Jack.'

I grabbed Neil by the shoulders, and to my surprise he gave in weakly, stumbling back a step. 'Look, this is not nineteen-fifties America,' I said. 'You can't hitch a ride with some innocent farm boys, or jump on a freight train like a hobo. Nobody will pick you up out here. You'll be walking all night.'

He shrugged. 'Then I'll find a spot to shelter, and continue in the morning. It's the way people travelled for centuries, Jack, before there were motorways, service stations and intercity trains. They used their two feet, their courage and their initiative, and they didn't die. They reached their destination in the end, and along the way they experienced the journey as you can never experience it when you're cruising along in a comfortable car with climate control and cruise control and windscreen wipers scraping away at any trace of natural life that might cloud your vision.'

'I can't leave you out here,' I said.

'Then join me.'

'It's too dangerous. Tomorrow, maybe. Let's go back to Oban and sit in a pub and talk about it, and at least then head out in the right direction.'

'Then what, Jack? Tour around looking at churches? Then get bored and go to India or Thailand or Guatemala? Then get bored with that and climb Everest or trek to the North Pole or bungee jump down the Grand Canyon? It wouldn't make a bit of difference. It would just be a longer and more expensive way to arrive at the same cul-de-sac.'

We talked on at each other for another ten minutes in the pouring rain, Neil telling me to take a risk and me refusing.

'You can't live until you've given up everything,' he kept insisting. 'Everyone from Jesus to Buddha to Tolstoy to Gandhi to Lao

Tsu has tried to tell us that, but we pay no attention because it's difficult. Well, living a shell of a life is difficult too, far too difficult for me.'

I told him not to be so melodramatic, and he told me I was shallow, and I told him he was a charlatan, and he called me a coward and I called him a poser, and he tramped off sullenly into the night, and I didn't even watch him go. I ran back into the warmth of the car, span it around and drove straight back to Oban, cursing him all the way.

At first I went to Eileen's B&B, and sat outside for ten minutes with the engine running, planning what I could say to persuade her to come with me to save Neil from himself. I could see her peeping out at me from behind a net curtain on the first floor, and at that moment I despised her with all my soul. I rehearsed line after line but I knew it was hopeless. She had more resolve than I did, and less courage. She would not go out into the night looking for Neil one more time. She was finished with him and, in any case, he was finished with her. If he wouldn't come with me, he certainly wouldn't go with her.

I drove from there down to the ferry terminal, for no logical reason. I parked in the big, empty car park, walked out in the cold to look at the schedule, which I knew perfectly well would say that there were no more boats going anywhere until the morning. I looked out to sea, where lights twinkled on the shore of Mull, and thought of Nicola far beyond in windy Barra, with her ruined carpet and scarred floor and charred first-edition Woolf. I thought of her going to bed in that cold house, perhaps hugging a pillow for comfort, or perhaps laid out drunk in an armchair. Perhaps, she was crying as well, although not for me. I wanted to go back and bury myself in her smooth, soft neck again, without what came after. I wanted the warmth of her, without the memory of Neil. But you can never go back, and I, it seems, can never go forward either. I turned and went back to my car, and spent another ten minutes driving aimlessly around Oban looking for something to do.

Eventually I found my way to an old ivy-strewn pub, ordered a scotch, downed it, ordered another, downed it, ordered another and sat feeling my throat burn and wondering what I would do with my life now that Neil Blake had wandered off into the night. Nothing came to mind. I seemed to fit in nowhere; Barra was dead for me, York held no appeal, while London was like a vast dirty blanket laid out ready to smother me. I certainly didn't belong in this twee little pub of genteel locals and middle-aged tourists, most of whom were too absorbed in themselves to care if I fell of the edge of the Earth, while a few of them glanced anxiously, seeing my anger and madness and hoping it wouldn't translate into an unpleasant scene.

I took out my notebook from my pocket and tried to write. Stories about Neil swarmed in my head, but when I wrote them down they sounded stupid. I was back in the hell of my novel again, censoring before I had written, crossing out and rewriting and crossing out and rewriting. I scratched angrily at the page, hunched over the table in a concentrated fury. Nothing good would come. I felt a rage building inside me but it had no outlet. I had nobody to talk to and nothing to do. I couldn't write, I couldn't read, and I didn't really want to drink. I was alone and rootless; I didn't have a place to stay, and the thought of driving alone through the night back to London was oppressive. With Neil I could have managed it as a mad scheme, but mad schemes seem pointless on your own.

I finished my scotch and slammed it down angrily on the table, breaking the pleasant murmur of conversation for a moment while eyes flitted towards me surreptitiously. I was disappointed: I'd hoped the glass would break. I stalked off into the dark slick streets and walked aimlessly. There were few cars out now. The last bus chugged down the high street with nobody aboard, and a bit later an ambulance burst past with blue lights flashing but siren dimmed so as not to disturb the peace of the dead-quiet town. Even the jet that flew overhead did so silently, its lights blinking in meek apology. Somewhere a dog barked. Then all was silent again.

The rain had slowed to a steady drizzle. I thought of Neil out there on that lonely road, and of all the nonsense he had talked, and I kept wondering if he was right and then dismissing the thought just as quickly. Neil was no Buddha. He had assimilated some disparate strands of philosophy but had no idea how to apply them. Whatever Lao Tsu was trying to say, he didn't seem to be advocating a wild step off into the unknown, abandoning everything and trusting to blind luck or fate to save oneself from ruin.

But Neil was obstinate. He would not listen to me. Nor would he be gone from my head. As far as he walked down that long, empty, winding coast road, he would no more be out of my head than if he walked to the North Pole. When I saw the rain slow I thought of how it would make him more comfortable.

When I saw cars heading south, I hoped they would pick him up. When I looked at my watch I counted the hours that Neil had been out there in the cold.

And I realised that if I abandoned him now, I would simply be counting the days, the weeks, the months and the years. I would think of Neil every time I slipped the Figaro into top gear, every time I ate a kebab or got stuck at a traffic light on the Holloway Road. He was in me, like a cancer, and no amount of scotch or walking in the rain would exorcise him. I got in the car and headed south.

14

I don't go to the Holloway Road anymore. I don't eat at Donna's Kebabs or mingle with the sweaty crowds in the Dog's Head. I don't cruise around in my Figaro watching the people stagger past. Even the old men's pubs and young mothers' cafés of Crouch End are too far away for me. I spend my days in the bedroom where I lived as a child. My computer is at a desk facing the wall. I switch it on every morning and switch it off at night. My mother cooks my meals and washes my clothes. My long literary novel is no nearer to completion than it was a year ago today, when I first met Neil Blake in a seedy kebab shack on the Holloway Road.

My mother smiles bravely at breakfast and asks me what I will do today. 'Nothing,' I reply, as I reply every morning. What is there to do? I look around London and see a vast grey graveyard. The concrete office towers and housing estates are monuments without epitaphs, because those trapped inside them will work and die without doing anything worthy of an epitaph. Most people would say living and working, but I think of them as dying. Working and dying in those big concrete gravestones. It's all a matter of perspective.

I tried getting a job and paying my own way, but I was not a success at anything. When my bosses told me about the great importance of the forms I would fill out and the dire consequences if I filed them in the wrong place, I laughed at them and made the sort of speech that would have made Neil proud, a pseudo-philosophical rambling discourse about the unreality of everything we perceive as real. I was quickly fired.

After one or two such experiences, I had no references to give, as the few acquaintances who recommended me out of consideration for my poor mother or my dead father now shied away. Even simple manual labour I found hard to get, and could not stick to when I got it. Work of any kind requires a basic commitment to the world that I now seem to lack. My tired glassy eyes see my own existence as unimportant, so how can they care about getting to work at nine o'clock instead of nine-thirty?

Even my mother rarely speaks to me now. We eat together most days, but hardly raise our eyes from our plates. She doesn't want to talk about my days with Neil — she tries to pretend that he never existed. But I know he did, and I know he's more real to me than anything else. There's nothing else I want to talk about, and so we just listen to the harsh scrape of forks on plates and the loud, wet motion of food around our mouths. Sometimes we might discuss who's doing the washing up, or she might ask me what I'm doing or try to persuade me to try some new job, but it's all just noise, no different from the chewing of our food or the scrape of forks on plates.

I have retreated to my bedroom, the refuge of years past. I have completed the circle. My life seems somehow to have run its course, and at the end of it I have arrived where I started, and know the place for the first time. Where before I felt oppressed and dreamt of following roads across Britain to new places and sights, now I am happy here, content with my narrow boundaries and certain routine. There are no surprises here. Perhaps I am living a shell of a life, but it is enough for me. Indeed, it is all I can live.

If I ventured out onto the Holloway Road, I might see him again, like Banquo bursting into a kebab shop or dive bar. I might be forced again to think of that dark, rain-streaked evening on the outskirts of Oban, when I drove south to look for Neil and found blue flashing lights by the side of the road where I'd left him an hour earlier. Strange that when the ambulance flashed through town I thought not of him. The rain made me think of him, the cars, the night and my own watch made me think of him. But not the ambulance. Neil, to me, was an immortal or, at the very least, an Achilles or Hector. In the strange, absurd event that he would die, it would have to be in heroic fashion, in a knife fight or a shootout or a dramatic plunge off a sky-high cliff. Nothing as banal as a traffic accident. It wasn't possible.

Even when I saw the blue lights, I expected to see Neil hopping up and down with boundless energy and excitedly regaling the paramedics with the long winding story of how he saw exactly what happened from the very beginning to the very end and could tell them all the details, if only they would just stop and listen. But, as it turned out, he probably didn't see a thing. He was probably just clipped from behind and knocked into the muddy gutter like a stray traffic cone. Or perhaps he heard the lorry coming, the first in hours, and jumped excitedly forward to wave it down thinking that, after all his sacrifice to the elements, the universe had provided for him after all.

For a split-second, he may even have

thought of how, when he got to where he was going, he would tell me how wrong I was, how his abandonment of everything worldly had been rewarded after all. Perhaps the fatigue of those wet, cold hours on the road affected his judgement, so he realised too late that he was too far out into the road, that the headlights were too bright, that the lorry was not slowing. Perhaps he realised in time, but decided that this, too, was the will of the universe. Or perhaps he was simply clipped from behind and tumbled into the mud, not knowing a thing about it.

When I slowed down and stopped by the side of the road, there was no fear in my head, even as I scanned the crowd for Neil and saw only paramedics in fluorescent jackets. Even when I saw the stretcher with a lumpy shape under the red blanket, I thought not of him. I still looked around, wondering if he had found a ride after all, planning to drive on after him as soon as I had found out what had happened here. I may even have thought about telling him all about it, the coincidence of this strange gathering just where I had left him. He loved stories, after all, and it wasn't fair that he was the only one to tell them. I wondered sometimes why he put up with me shuffling along beside him, not contributing anything while he gave everything. And so it was with something like eagerness that I approached the nearest paramedic and asked what had happened.

'Would you move along, please, sir,' he said. 'Just a nasty accident, nothing to see.'

Then a colleague of his looked across and grabbed his arm. They conferred for a while, glancing at me. Strange as it seems, I think that even then I did not suspect what they were about to tell me. I waited dumbly for information, not imagining for a moment that they were about to rub Neil out of my life, and so to end it. Then they turned to me and I saw a little gold locket, and in it was a passport photo, and it was me and Neil in a booth somewhere on the Holloway Road, laughing at a joke I could no longer remember.

'Have you seen this before?'

'No,' I said, thinking the man meant the locket, which I had truly never seen. Such an absurd thing, a locket. It was something you might find in one of Oscar's romances, nestling softly in a heaving bosom. But the photo, yes, I remembered the photo, or at least I remembered having it taken. There were two, and I had the other one, although I didn't know where it had got to and despite much searching I have never found it since. But Neil had kept his in a ridiculous old locket that he must have picked up at some antique stall or junkyard in one of the many towns he had drifted through. I cried a little, not because Neil was dead — I still hadn't realised that — but because he had kept his photo of us close to his heart and I had lost mine. I had let him down, as I always let him down. The paramedic put an arm around my shoulder to stop me crying, but he didn't realise that I still didn't know.

Then finally, as I stood staring at the red lump under the blanket, I began to realise that Neil was not a god, or a hero. He was not even Dean Moriarty, and Dean Moriarty was not even Neal Cassady, and Neal Cassady was no more than a man anyway. The ideas I had got into my head about Neil were just ideas. He was mortal flesh, and he had died. Absurd, really, that I could have thought anything else. But when you heard him speaking those long fervent sentences that wound on for ages without a breath, you'd swear he was The Word itself. But he wasn't. He was flesh, and flesh he always had been. And now he was dead.

I must have stumbled a bit, because the paramedics were then supporting me and ushering me over to sit on the roadway on the other side of the ambulance from that lumpy red blanket. They were saying things to me, but it didn't really matter what. They had already said the last thing that would ever matter to me. Neil was dead. After that I went through various formalities, which I scarcely noticed at the time and don't remember now. I don't even know how I got back to London. I don't know if my Figaro is still parked out there on the muddy edge of a lonely road winding down the Scottish coast to a grand old dead end. I don't care. I have no use for it now.

So now I live in grey ugly London with the other dead and dying souls. I don't even go out and mingle with them — I can't muster the energy for the pretence. Like my dull relatives, whom I now see much more often and find less intolerable, I am already dead. Whether the final medical confirmation comes a year or seventy years from now is unimportant. The means may hold some interest, I suppose. Cancer may claim me, or the sweet circular irony of a traffic accident. Or, if I get truly impatient, Suicide Bridge is not far away. It arcs over the A1, an optimistic Victorian innovation now serving as a hot spot for depressed teenagers looking to end it all with a few seconds in the air, the sweet smack of tarmac and the juddering wheels of an articulated lorry crushing any doubt.

I have thought of it often in these last few months. The idea of dying on the A1, where Neil once stuck his head out of my Figaro and yelled at commuters at the sweet hopeful beginning of our great road trip, seems at times strangely appropriate, at others a little contrived. Such a dramatic gesture is best reserved for those teenagers still bursting with life even in their last few windswept seconds clinging to the railing. For those, like me, who are already dead, it seems redundant. Better, I think, to wait for the slight surprise of discovering the day and the hour.

In the meantime, I sit in my childhood bedroom in my mother's old house in Crouch End. In the morning I switch on my computer, open up my huge sprawling novel and shuffle a few passages around. Sometimes I delete some, and replace them with a passage about Neil. Slowly my novel gets shorter, and simpler, and loses its literary credentials, and becomes reminiscent of that great paean to the American soul to which Neil and I listened as we toured around Britain. Soon there will be nothing of the original left. Neil will have taken it over. It will be the story of a young British man pursuing an American dream, stubbornly refusing to accept that dreams are dreams and will remain forever so. When the waking mind tries to grasp the dream, it slips away into the night. Better to leave dreams for the night-time, and to sleepwalk through the day accepting the chains that bind you. That's what I do. In fact, these days I hardly even sleepwalk. I just sit in my bedroom and type. I find that if you stay really still, you start to forget the chains are even there.

Sometimes, when I go to my window and look out at the grey north London rooftops, I think of Neil. I look at Alexandra Palace gleaming on the hill, the red-brick chimneys, the grey concrete blocks full of people dreaming, living, eating and slowly dying, the bustling little Broadway with its shops and cafés and its pavements clogged with prams, the clock tower built to preserve the memory of some long-forgotten local hero, the rows of houses like furrowed earth on the broad Iowa plains, the big open sky above calling to something bigger and less squalid, and I think of Neil Blake reaching for that something even though he had no idea what it was and no chance whatsoever of getting it. I think of Neil Blake stretching the narrow little confines of Britain to breaking point, I think of old Neil Blake, the god who fell to earth and turned out to be a man after all, battered and broken under a red blanket on a windswept muddy road, I think of Neil Blake dreaming and striving and refusing to die before he had lived, I think of Neil Blake holding my hand in the icy North Sea under a million watching stars. I think of Neil Blake.

We do hope that you have enjoyed reading this large print book.

Did you know that all of our titles are available for purchase?

We publish a wide range of high quality large print books including:
Romances, Mysteries, Classics
General Fiction
Non Fiction and Westerns

Special interest titles available in large print are:
The Little Oxford Dictionary
Music Book
Song Book
Hymn Book
Service Book

Also available from us courtesy of Oxford University Press:
Young Readers' Dictionary
(large print edition)
Young Readers' Thesaurus
(large print edition)

For further information or a free brochure, please contact us at:
Ulverscroft Large Print Books Ltd.,
The Green, Bradgate Road, Anstey,
Leicester, LE7 7FU, England.
Tel: (00 44) **0116 236 4325**
Fax: (00 44) **0116 234 0205**

Other titles published by
The House of Ulverscroft:

TRUE MURDER

Yaba Badoe

Eleven-year-old Ajuba has been abandoned at a Devon boarding school by her Ghanaian father. Haunted by the circumstances of her mother's breakdown and her life in Ghana, she falls under the spell of new girl Polly Venus and her family. But all is not what it seems in the Venus household and Ajuba can only watch as the family tear itself apart. One day the girls find the bones of a dead baby wrapped up in an old coat in the attic of the Venus manor house. Obsessed with the detectives of the American magazine serial *True Murder*, the girls set out to find out what happened to the baby and as the summer draws to a close, three tragedies conflate, with catastrophic results.

LEFTOVERS

Laura Wiess

Forgiveness is far off for teenagers Blair and Ardith, best friends and accomplices in a terrible crime. At the home of the only adult they trust, a police officer, the girls confess every horrifying detail. But it becomes clear the act wasn't out of malice or revenge, but born of fierce loyalty and unimaginable desperation. Written off by abusive parents and mocked and shunned by their classmates, Blair and Ardith had found a safe haven with one another. And when that haven was threatened, they knew they must do everything in their power to protect it. Whatever the cost.

TRAVEL WRITING

Peter Ferry

Pete Ferry is driving home when a car, swerving dangerously on the road, overtakes him. The driver is a beautiful woman, half-naked — something's clearly not right. Cautiously, he follows her. What should he do? Then, at the traffic light, he's next to her car. He must act now — but he hesitates, the lights change and her car lurches forward straight into a tree, killing her instantly . . . In Chicago, Pete tells this story to the students in his class where he teaches. But, is this just an elaborate tale which illustrates the power of storytelling? Or did this actually happen?

FAMILY PLANNING

Karan Mahajan

Mr Ahuja, Minister for Urban Development, is beset by problems: his daily struggle over whether to resign for the sixty-third time; thirteen children; his pregnant wife, Sangita, seemingly adrift on a sea of knitting and nappies; his son Rishi and his maddening serial apologies . . . and finally there's Arjun, the wisest of his sprawling family. However, even Arjun feels defeated: how does he tell the girl on the school bus that he's crazy about her? And Arjun's father must confront the roots of his strange and disturbing marriage in the troubled landscape of modern-day New Delhi that he himself has built.

HAMMER

Sara Stockbridge

Grace Hammer lives a sweet enough life with her children in London's dank and dirty East End, dipping the pockets of wealthy strangers foolish enough to enter there. She keeps a clean house and a tight hold on her magpie nature, restricting her interests to wallets and pocket watches. At night she dreams of shiny things. Out in the dark countryside Mr Blunt rocks in his seat by the fire, grinding his teeth. He has never forgotten his scarlet treasure, or the harlot who stole it from him. At night he dreams of slitting her lily-white throat . . .

A TOWN CALLED IMMACULATE

Peter Anthony

It's Christmas Eve, and when bankrupt farmer Ray Marak saves the life of his friend and banker, Josh Werther, neither they nor their neighbours can imagine what the night will bring. Still traumatized by his time in Vietnam, Ray's world has shrunk — to the boundaries of his home town of Immaculate, and the warmth of his family: his sons Jacob and Ethan, and his wife Renee; Renee, the woman who waited for him during his wartime hell. But as the snow accumulates, so do the townspeople's stories, and the suspicions Ray has harboured for years start to resurface.